A LADY'S PRIDE

A Pride and Prejudice Retelling

Jennifer Kay

For Charlotte

This work is, of course, based on Jane Austen's masterpiece, and I have taken the liberty of adapting some of her original dialogue to meet my version of the story. I do not claim to own that writing, nor do I claim the original plot ideas reproduced in this novel. Any mistakes are my own.

Chapter One

Elizabeth Bennet was *not* enjoying the Netherfield ball. To say she was miserable would have been a false statement, for Elizabeth was not a creature built for misery. Still, the evening she had anticipated had disappeared only seconds after she had passed through the front door, and Elizabeth felt its loss keenly.

If only Mr. Collins had stayed at home! Mary's botched expedition on the pianoforte could be ignored; Lydia and Kitty's shameless flirting with every officer present was horrid, but nothing she hadn't dealt with before. Her mother's blatant encouragement of her youngest two daughters and her father's laughter over them all were similarly familiar.

Her cousin, however, fell into a league all by himself. His dancing was so atrocious that Elizabeth couldn't fathom why his dear patron Lady Catherine hadn't long ago forbid him from partaking in the sport. Sadly, though, crushed toes and jarring collisions paled in comparison to the conversation. During their dance, Mr. Collins kept up a constant stream of remarks about the generosity of the hosts, the grandness of the room—although it was nothing compared to Rosings Park, of course—and his own vastly exaggerated attributes.

When at long last the song ended, Elizabeth limped away to join her friend Charlotte Lucas.

"My goodness, Lizzy, you'd think we were at a funeral rather than a ball," Charlotte remarked, smiling. "He couldn't have been that bad, honestly."

"Worse," Elizabeth declared stoutly, but the exchange brought a begrudging smile to her lips. "I fear my feet are too damaged to even contemplate another dance tonight. No, Charlotte, I shall content myself with watching Jane and Bingley fall even more in love and dream up all the tricks I can teach their children."

Charlotte laughed. "The children of those two wouldn't get up to tricks, Lizzy. They wouldn't know how!" She looked around, then lowered her voice even more than it already was. "But if she wants children, if she wants *him*, she ought to be more obvious about it! You know how she feels, but does he?"

Elizabeth sat back, affronted. "Be more obvious! If he can't see her regard, then he is a fool. She has done nothing but encourage him tonight, ever since we first arrived!"

"She greeted him as the host and has treated half a dozen other men to her smiles since then, Lizzy."

"This is Jane we are talking about," Elizabeth retorted, remembering only at the last moment to keep her voice at a whisper. "She smiles at everybody, it is who she is! If they are to marry, shouldn't he know her well enough to realize that?"

Charlotte had started shaking her head halfway through the comment. "She ought to move fast, snatch him up. There will be plenty of time for smiles and getting to know each other after the wedding. There are plenty of strangers who have happy marriages, Lizzy. In fact, it may be easier to find happiness marrying a stranger, for you have no expectations that way."

Elizabeth's protest at the notion was cut off by the sudden appearance of Mr. Darcy. He gave Charlotte a solicitous nod, then turned and bowed to Elizabeth. "Might I inquire for your hand in the next dance, Miss Elizabeth?"

Caught off guard and still in a state of agitation from the previous conversation, Elizabeth found herself in the rare situation of being at a loss for words. Finally, she managed to stammer, "You may, Mr. Darcy."

He bowed again and walked away, leaving Elizabeth to wonder what had just happened and why on earth she had told him yes, especially when she had the perfectly good excuse of crushed toes.

Charlotte, always practical, did not seem much perturbed. "No doubt you will find him more agreeable in private conversation. Some men are like that."

Elizabeth bit back the jab that Charlotte could hardly have had much experience with men at the last moment, closing her teeth onto her tongue and wincing. At that fortuitous moment, the notes of the previous song faded and the dancers began pairing up with new partners.

"Don't be a fool, Lizzy," Charlotte whispered. "He is of ten times Wickham's consequence."

"And ten times more disagreeable," Elizabeth retorted as she stood and smoothed her skirts. Oh, *why* had she said yes?

Darcy said nothing as he led her onto the floor and they took their places. He was silent as the musicians played the opening chords and remained so for long enough that Elizabeth began to wonder if he meant to say anything at all during their entire dance.

"I am surprised you asked me to dance, Mr. Darcy," she said after considering several other barbs. "If you simply meant to observe me with silent disdain, you could have done so from across the room at much less inconvenience to yourself."

He looked taken aback, and Elizabeth felt a surge of accomplishment for making him lose his ever-present façade.

"Do you always exchange insults in a ballroom, Miss Elizabeth?" he asked after a moment, seeming to regain his calm demeanor.

"No," she said pertly, and then the dance separated them for several measures. When they came together again she went on, "But one must speak a little, you know. Can you imagine how strange it would look to go an entire half-hour without exchanging a single word?" She broke away again and turned back to find him watching her with the hint of an amused expression on his face. Instantly annoyed, she added, "Although for some, the conversation ought to be arranged so they need not trouble themselves to say more than half a dozen words."

"Are you consulting your own feelings in the present case, or do you imagine that you are gratifying mine?"

Oh, no, she would never *gratify his feelings*. She was not Caroline Bingley, to fawn over his every word in constant hope that he could be swayed into matrimony by flattery.

"Both," replied Elizabeth archly; "for I have always seen a great similarity in the turn of our minds. We are each of an unsocial, taciturn disposition, unwilling to speak, unless we expect to say something that will amaze the whole room, and be handed down to posterity with all the éclat of a proverb."

"I wonder if you believe any of that as it regards yourself," Darcy remarked, looking down at her intently as the dance brought them together. "Undoubtedly you think it a true portrait of my character."

"I have my pride, Mr. Darcy," she quipped, thinking of his comment on the eve of their first meeting, when he had declared her *tolerable, but not handsome enough to tempt him.* "It has less basis than yours, to be sure, but I like to believe I am listened to when I open my mouth. As for *your* pride, that has never been in doubt! I believe all of Meryton is acquainted with it."

The lines around his mouth tightened, and Elizabeth claimed the movement as another victory. If he meant to glare at her continually, she could repay him with verbal barbs and see how he liked feeling uncomfortable for a change!

"Tell me, do you and your sisters often walk to Meryton?" he asked after a pause.

"We do," she replied steadily. "It is a pleasant diversion and puts us in the way of new people. In fact, when you met us there the other day, we had just been forming a new acquaintance."

This time it was his whole face that tightened in anger. "Ah, yes. Mr. Wickham has made yet another conquest in you and your sisters. I would have thought you had better sense."

"On the contrary, I found him to be a pleasant, well-spoken man."

He was definitely struggling to keep his temper in check now. "Mr. Wickham is blessed with such happy manners as may ensure his making friends— whether he may be equally capable of retaining them, is less certain."

"He has been so unlucky as to lose your friendship," Elizabeth all but snapped, "and in a manner he is likely to suffer from all his life."

"Yes, I'm sure he told *you*, for all intents and purposes a stranger, of his many misfortunes in great detail," Darcy said, his lips now rimmed in white as he pressed them together.

The insinuation that she lacked discernment sent a flash of anger through Elizabeth, and she replied hardly without knowing what she said, "Better to be blinded by kindness and compassion than by unwarranted prejudice, don't you think, Mr. Darcy?"

"Do you ask because you desire my opinion, or have you already determined what I think with no need of input from me?"

"Do you allow yourself to be blinded by prejudice, Mr. Darcy?" Elizabeth asked, leveling her gaze at him. The steps of the dance brought them close together at that moment, and she stumbled slightly, feeling overwhelmed for a moment and immediately kicking herself for losing her cool demeanor. Somewhere, surely, Caroline Bingley was laughing at her mistake. While Elizabeth was not bothered a bit by the lady's opinion of her, she very much cared that her stumble might have shown Mr. Darcy how invested she was in their conversation.

"I try not to be," he replied, and her brain took a moment to remember the question he had answered. "Of course, I can hardly expect to view my own actions without some bias, no matter how much I may endeavor to try." A pause, and then he continued, "Is there a purpose behind your questions, Miss Elizabeth? I had not thought you the type of woman to come at a problem from the side when it could be addressed head-on."

Oh yes, he must think she was quite headstrong and therefore unladylike—so different than his meek, accomplished sister who seemed to bring him such pride. "I am merely attempting to make out your character, Mr. Darcy," she said.

He looked vaguely relieved. "And how do you get on?"

"Very poorly," she told him frankly. "I hear such different accounts of you that as soon as I think I have made up my mind I must change it again. You puzzle me exceedingly, sir."

"I understand that accounts of my behavior can vary greatly," he replied, "and I would beg of you to withhold your final decision at the moment, for the result would likely not reflect on either of us in our best light. I could not bear, for you especially—"

A shriek sliced through the room like a knife, followed by a crash and several dull thuds of varying magnitude. The music ground to a ragged halt and all the couples turned immediately towards the sound. They parted in a way that gave Elizabeth a direct view of what had caused the commotion, and the sight made her knees give way. Not ten feet away, just off the dance floor, her father lay splayed across the floor. He was not moving.

For several long moments, the world lost its focus as waves of shock and horror washed over her. The only sound in her ears was a faint buzzing, the only sensation she felt was the thudding of her own heart.

Slowly, the world re-formed around her, and Elizabeth became aware that she had collapsed forward into Mr. Darcy, and his strong grip on her elbows was the only thing keeping her from sliding to

9

the floor. Somewhere in the back of her mind she felt dismay at looking so weak before a man she despised, but that sensation was far-off as well, something to be dealt with at a later time.

The next thing to enter her awareness was the sound of her own ragged breathing—gasps, really— as she fought to keep her composure. That was followed by a low but insistent voice repeating her name. "Miss Elizabeth. Miss Elizabeth, look at me. All will be well. Elizabeth."

The last word, with its inherent intimacy, shocked her into looking up. Mr. Darcy's dark eyes held hers, and for once she could read his expression. Concern made his entire face look different, she noted in the same distant portion of her mind. "All will be well," he repeated, his voice taking on a tone she had never heard him use before.

"No," she whispered. Then the rest of the world came flooding back in—her mother's continued shrieks, the shout issued by some man to send for a doctor, the cacophony of voices raised all around her. No, if her father died it most assuredly would not be alright. Shoving away from Mr. Darcy, Elizabeth stumbled shakily across the several feet of dance floor and threw herself to her knees besides her father.

Chapter Two

If Darcy hadn't had reason to think ill of her family previously, Elizabeth reflected later, he certainly did as the events following Mr. Bennet's collapse played out. Mrs. Bennet wailed ceaselessly, alternating between pleas for help and announcing that they were destitute, all of them, and would be turned out of Longbourn with nowhere to go.

Mary peered down at her father, as if scared she too would collapse if she stood too close, and offered thoughts on his condition from books she had read. Since each idea usually ended in death, her words only heightened Mrs. Bennet's fervor. Lydia and Kitty also stood apart, but their exclamations tended in the same direction as Mrs. Bennet's. How would the officers visit them if they had nowhere to stay, or worse, had to leave Meryton for good?

Of all the Bennet sisters, Jane alone knelt on the floor next to Elizabeth. Lizzy held her father's hand gently on one side and Jane's tightly on the other as they waited for the doctor—luckily among the assembled guests—to deliver his prognosis. He had just declared that not all hope was lost, but Mr. Bennet required rest and quiet, when the worst transgression occurred.

Mr. Collins had also been hovering over Mr. Bennet as he was examined, alternating between trying to reassure Mrs. Bennet that all would be well and offering his services as a clergyman should they be called for. As the doctor sat back, however, his attentions turned elsewhere.

"This is a time of great trial and uncertainty," he began, looking out at the group around him as Elizabeth imagined he surveyed the world from his pulpit, "and it pleases me to do my duty to offer what reassurances I can to those affected most. I have not known my cousins previously, but I have grown most fond of them during my visit, as I am sure any of you who know them cannot help but understand. I now announce that my true purpose in visiting Longbourn was to select from among my cousins the woman who will make me the happiest of men."

Elizabeth looked up slowly, her thoughts still focused on her father, to stare at her cousin in horror. How could he think such an announcement was appropriate at the moment? But Mr. Collins had not finished.

"While my intentions originally intended towards the oldest Miss Bennet, I have been informed that her heart is engaged elsewhere, and I can only wish her the happiest." He gave a solicitous nod towards Mr. Bingley, who to his credit was managing to keep his expression neutral throughout the speech. "So," Mr. Collins continued, "I have determined that Miss Elizabeth Bennet would make a most suitable bride, and I am pleased to offer my hand and the assurances that, should Mr. Bennet perish, there is no need for any of your sisters to leave Longbourn until the event occurs in the natural way."

At long last, he turned towards Elizabeth, who was struggling in vain to keep her face calm. Mr. Collins opened his mouth to speak on, but Elizabeth, knowing she would create a far greater scene if he should continue in such a vein, burst out, "Oh, do not talk of such things, sir! This cannot be the time—I cannot bear to think of home without my father while there is a chance he may recover. Speak no more, I beg of you!"

"But Cousin Elizabeth—" Mr. Collins began, looking quite offended that his stilted proposal had not been met with grateful overtures.

To Elizabeth's surprise, it was Mr. Darcy who came to her rescue. "The lady is correct. It is hardly suitable to speak of a man's death while ignoring his needs in life. Surely you would not wish to stop Mr. Bennet from receiving the care he needs presently."

The statement was delivered with the haughtiest visage Elizabeth had seen on the man yet, but in that moment Darcy's stern face was her saving grace. Mr. Collins acquiesced at once, turning his attention to praising Mr. Darcy as "just as great as his aunt, the Lady Catherine, whom he had the greatest advantage to know as his patroness."

Darcy, seeming oblivious to the man, nodded at the doctor and several of the Bingley servants who had gathered. They moved forward immediately to complete the task of moving Mr. Bennet to a location better for resting than the ballroom floor. Distantly, Elizabeth heard Mr. Bingley issuing directions on where he was to be taken.

Standing to move out of the way, Elizabeth found herself near enough Miss Bingley to hear the woman remark to Mrs. Hurst, voice full of exasperation, "Dear me, are we to host every Bennet in turn while they recuperate? There is no chance now that we will be able to return to London tomorrow, Charles is far too kind-hearted for that."

"Perhaps Mr. Bennet will be well enough to return home in the morning," Mrs. Hurst replied. "We could be on our way to Town by noon."

"Well enough, or dead," Miss Bingley said viciously.

"Caroline!" Mrs. Hurst admonished, clearly shocked.

Elizabeth did not wait to hear more. The charged exchange with Mr. Darcy, her father's collapse, Mr. Collins' proposal, Miss Bingley's cruelty—it was all too much to take in at once. Turning, she searched the room for a way to escape. Surely there had to be somewhere private at Netherfield where she could collect herself before she broke down.

Keeping her head down as she moved towards the nearest exit, Elizabeth nearly collided with a large form. She looked up into Mr. Darcy's glaring face, even more severe than he had been when facing Mr. Collins. For a moment, Elizabeth simply stared up at him. Could it really have been just minutes ago that she was dancing, her primary concern in the world Mr. Wickham's fate? He opened his mouth to speak and she jerked back to her senses. Dropping her gaze, she darted around him and out of the room, leaving the chaos behind her as she fled.

&

The ladies of Longbourn returned home in the early hours of the morning. Mrs. Bennet had been making broad hints that all of them should stay on at Netherfield, and Elizabeth could only be thankful that she had returned to the group in time to persuade her mother otherwise. It took both herself and Jane to shepherd their mother and sisters out to the waiting carriage, but at last they were on their way home.

Even after agreeing that she herself would return to Longbourn, Mrs. Bennet tried valiantly to leave Jane behind until the carriage wheels began to turn. Since Mr. Bingley had sent for a nurse, however, there was no reason for her to stay, and so she joined the rest of the party.

"I am surprised you do not try to stay, Miss Eliza," Miss Bingley said with an overly-sweet smile as they approached the carriage. "You were such a dedicated nurse to your poor sister when she took ill, and I have heard it said that you are your father's favorite. Perhaps the sentiment does not run both ways?"

Elizabeth did not bother to look at Miss Bingley, but instead addressed Mr. Bingley. "I will not presume to invade your home, Mr. Bingley, but I should dearly like to visit my father later today. I am sure the nurse is most capable, but I will feel better if I am able to see him for myself on occasion."

"Of course, Miss Elizabeth," Mr. Bingley replied. "You are welcome to visit him as often as you like, as are your sisters."

Luckily they stood somewhat apart from the rest of the Bennet party at that time, and Mrs. Bennet could not turn the invitation to her advantage. "I thank you. I will certainly come, and may bring Jane with me. I must confess that my younger sisters' aptitude for nursing leaves something to be desired, but Mary may join us as well." She looked to the waiting carriage, where the rest of her family already sat. "Excuse me, Mr. Bingley. I thank you for the ball, and for ensuring my father's comfort. I shall pray that he recovers as fully as Jane did under your roof."

She curtseyed and went to the carriage. Mr. Collins, who should have waited to hand her up as the sole male in the party, had already seated himself. Elizabeth knew herself to be perfectly capable of getting into a carriage, but the oversight stung. And this man wanted to be her husband! She had just made up her mind to climb in unaided when Mr. Darcy stepped up and extended his hand. "Miss Elizabeth."

She curtseyed and accepted his assistance, not meeting his eyes. No doubt he and Miss Bingley would enjoy ridiculing the whole lot of them once they were out of earshot. "Mr. Darcy."

"Oh, Jane, you should have stayed!" Mrs. Bennet wailed as they turned out of Netherfield's drive onto the main road. "I had so hoped that Mr. Bingley would propose last night, in fact I was sure of it, and I do not doubt that he would have if the situation had been different. Oh, why did Mr. Bennet collapse? What is to become of you? What is to become of all of us?"

"It hardly would have been appropriate to propose after Papa collapsed, if he indeed meant to do so,"

Jane replied steadily. "Papa will have to give his consent, after all."

Mrs. Bennet continued to protest, but Elizabeth quit listening. At some point Mr. Collins joined the conversation, droning on with little chance for anyone else to speak, but Elizabeth ignored him too. Jane's words had brought back the horror of last night's proposal, and with the memory came a knot of dread that settled deep in her stomach.

When at long last they reached Longbourn, Elizabeth practically threw herself from the carriage and, pleading a headache from the long night, hurried past the waiting servants and up the stairs to her room. Barely managing to not slam the door behind her, she removed her shoes and stockings and threw them aside, then discarded her dress with only slightly more care.

Standing at the window in only her shift, she stared out over the familiar landscape. Of course she had always known that one day Longbourn would cease to be her home. The entail on the estate was likewise a fact of life, often bemoaned by her mother but still never questioned. But oh, how shocking it was to consider leaving! As for life without her father, Elizabeth could not bear to think about such a world. Yet both situations hovered over her, ready to crash down at any moment.

If Mr. Collins proposed before the ball, or in any other situation, Elizabeth would have turned him down the second he allowed her to reply. But if—oh, God, it hurt to even consider it—should her father die, Elizabeth did not delude herself about the situation she and her sisters would be in. There was no extra money, no small home purchased and put aside for such an occurrence. With nowhere to go and no source of income, they would be hard pressed to find decent husbands. Mrs. Bennet might convince herself that Jane marrying Mr. Bingley would solve the problem, but Elizabeth had her doubts that the event would ever take place. Even if it did, they could not expect Mr. Bingley to house all four of his wife's sisters and her mother indefinitely.

The door opened behind her and Jane entered, her light step immediately recognizable even through Elizabeth's distress. *Poor Jane.* Her sweet, selfless older sister deserved a secure home and life. Jane, who had more reason than any of her other sisters to bemoan the events of the ball, would no doubt end up comforting all of them. How could she let Jane lose her home and her opportunity for happiness with Mr. Bingley?

Standing in the predawn light at her window, Elizabeth clearly saw what she must do. For the good of her family, for *Jane*, she had to accept Mr. Collins' proposal.

But for her own sake, how could she?

Chapter Three

Despite the events of the previous night, Elizabeth arose at her usual early hour. She slipped out of bed, careful to not wake Jane, and donned a simple dress. Carrying her shoes, Elizabeth made her way down the stairs and into the kitchen. Even on a normal day, both Mrs. Bennet and Mr. Collins slept late, but today Elizabeth would take no chances.

Mrs. Hill, the housekeeper, was awake and going about her duties as if there had been no disturbance the night before as well. She greeted Elizabeth quietly, the lack of her usual smile the only sign that something was terribly wrong. "Will you be going for your walk today, Miss Elizabeth?"

Elizabeth nodded mutely. She too lacked her customary smile.

"Okay. It will be a quiet house for hours yet. Take care, miss."

"I always am," Elizabeth responded. She finished putting her shoes on and stood up, shaking out her skirts. "Don't worry if I'm gone for some time. I may walk to Netherfield to see Papa."

"I'll pray for good news," Mrs. Hill said.

Elizabeth gave her a wan smile and escaped out the side door. The cool, clear morning air washed over her like a balm, and she breathed in deeply. The pit of worry remained lodged in her stomach, but in the morning light it seemed to weigh somewhat less.

She struck out in the direction of Netherfield, choosing to take the road rather than going through the fields as she had done when Jane was ill. Likely the inhabitants of Netherfield would not be awake for some time yet; there was no need to hurry. Of course, there was the chance that Mr. Darcy was already awake. During her stay at Netherfield, he had often been the only inhabitant to reach the breakfast room before her.

Thinking of the man brought back the unsettling memories of their dance and her hands clenched automatically in response. Never before had she danced—or simply conversed—with a man who made her feel so judged for who she was and what she said. The image of his white-lipped face came to mind. Did he look down on her for daring to prefer a soldier to a man who had ten thousand pounds a year, or was his anger over Wickham based on something else? Surely it must be a new idea to him that she would not accept his word as law just because society held him on a pedestal. And he had dared to suggest that she ought to clearly see the truth of the matter— *his* truth—without once offering a reason! Wretched, prideful man!

And then she had collapsed into him. God help her, what he must have thought! Elizabeth felt her cheeks heat at the memory and her fists tightened until her fingernails bit into her palms. Miss Bingley, ever watchful where Mr. Darcy was concerned, had undoubtedly noticed as well. Her family had made a grand fool of themselves last night, and Elizabeth felt the embarrassment keenly. If it wasn't for Jane and the happiness she could find with Mr. Bingley, Elizabeth would have been perfectly happy never setting eyes on anyone in the Netherfield party. She would face them today for her father's sake only, and do her best to ignore the disparaging remarks that were sure to come.

Elizabeth trudged on, taking far less joy from the walk than she normally did, but still managing to soothe her spirits enough that while she arrived at Netherfield feeling anxious, irritated, and tense, she nonetheless felt more like herself than she had since her father had collapsed.

She was shown in, feeling more than a little déjà vu. Having previously decided to ignore Miss Bingley's poor behavior, Elizabeth was unperturbed when the lady did not stand to greet her and instead burst out, "Goodness gracious, Miss Eliza, I had thought you would be more careful of your image following last night's events! I did not think your fiancé would allow such behavior to continue. Walking all the way from Longbourn without a chaperone, and through a town where the militia is quartered! You are bold indeed."

"He is not my fiancé until I accept his suit, Miss Bingley—*if* I accept his suit," Elizabeth replied calmly, "and I can hardly make a decision on such a matter when my father is unable to give his input. Has there been any change on his condition?"

"I do not know, I have not heard if there is. He is upstairs, the servant can show you the room."

Mr. Darcy, who had been silent throughout the exchange, stood. "I will show Miss Elizabeth to her father; I must return to my rooms in any case to retrieve the letter I am writing to Georgiana. She will need to be informed of our plans."

Miss Bingley burst into her usual effusions of praise for Darcy's sister and how much she missed seeing Miss Darcy, but Mr. Darcy merely acknowledged her with a nod and made his way across the room to where Elizabeth stood. "If you will follow me," he said, giving her a small bow and leading her out of the room.

They climbed the stairs in silence. Elizabeth stared fixedly at the back of his coat until they reached the top of the staircase and he turned slightly towards her.

"Do you agree with Miss Bingley, sir?" she asked suddenly.

"In what way, Miss Bennet? I believe Miss Bingley has professed a great deal of things in our shared company, and I cannot truthfully state to agree or disagree with all of them."

"That I ought not walk alone, Mr. Darcy. Do you find it shocking that a woman dares to transport herself in a manner that would never be questioned of a man?"

He frowned. "I do not believe you should be so careless with your walks, Miss Bennet. For a lady to walk unchaperoned at home, in a garden, is a pastime in which I see no harm. But to travel such a distance, and through an area full of soldiers, is something I firmly believe is not suitable for a lady."

"The soldiers have been nothing but gentlemen!" Elizabeth snapped. "I am in a place I have known since birth, surrounded by longtime acquaintances. Do your strictures apply to such a situation, Mr. Darcy?"

"Many men act the gentleman until given the situation to take advantage of a woman," Mr. Darcy said. "Or perhaps until a woman they have known as a child can no longer be called such. The fact that you believe elsewise shows your naiveté, and such a trait is not beneficial when making decisions on where to walk. I also confess I am surprised at you, Miss Elizabeth, for I had thought that despite how your sisters may behave, you cared about propriety and the consequences of your actions."

Mr. Darcy came to a stop before a door. "This is your father's room."

She glared up at him. "I thank you, sir, for both your assistance and your *worldly* opinions." Turning on her heel, she entered the room and closed the door.

Why, oh *why* did the man have to aggravate her so?

&

The next hour passed with little thought spared for Mr. Darcy. The nurse, a kindly woman named Mrs. Chrisley, was pleased to have her assistance, and Elizabeth made the most of the time to determine for herself how her father fared. Unfortunately, there was little for her to see. Her father lay still on the bed, propped up on pillows. His breathing was at once reassuringly steady and shockingly shallow, and while Elizabeth took heart from the pulse that beat like clockwork on his neck, the lack of movement left her spooked.

Never had she spent so long with her father that he had not offered a witty quip or some keen observation about their surroundings or the world at large. Even the hours they had spent together reading on long winter days had contained a sharing of ideas or discussion on a thought-provoking phrase.

And Mrs. Chrisley, while allaying many of Elizabeth's fears, was unable to dispel all of them.

"He may wake up or he may not, miss," she said frankly after Elizabeth asked at least a dozen questions about her father's health. "He's steady, which is always a good sign, and as you saw I've been able to give him liquids. There's no sign of fever. All you or I can do for him at the moment is keep him comfortable. The doctor mentioned that he still may be able to hear, so you're free to talk or read to him if you'd like, but I don't see what it will do. Of course, I've no great learning like the doctor."

"Would it bother you greatly if I read to him?" Elizabeth asked immediately. Her father never missed the daily paper, and if there was any chance he *could* still hear, well, this was one thing she could actually *do* for him. There were only so many times a person could re-plump pillows or run a cool cloth across his brow, and try though she might, Elizabeth knew that she would never have Jane's endless patience.

"Not at all, miss," the nurse replied. "Only there's nothing in here for you to read."

Elizabeth stood. "If you'll excuse me, I know where I can find what I need." She left the room on quick, quiet feet and headed directly for the library. While Netherfield boasted a study, she had never seen Mr. Bingley use it. In fact, the only person she had observed reading the paper at Netherfield was Mr. Darcy, and so she determined the most likely place to find the paper was next to his usual chair.

Her assumption was correct, and to her relief the room was empty. Tucking the paper under one arm and making a mental note to return it when she left, Elizabeth turned to make her way back up the stairs to her father.

She had not gone far when voices reached her. They came from the sitting room, and while Elizabeth hesitated at first only in surprise, she came to a full stop at the sound of her name.

"—does Miss Eliza *mean*, appearing yet again out of the wilds to nurse yet another one of her relatives who so conveniently fell ill at Netherfield. Does she believe that she is better equipped to provide care than a trained nurse? My brother ought to have spared himself the expense if Mr. Bennet's family insists on being here either way."

"That is Bingley's way, you could hardly expect him to do otherwise. I will allow that Miss

27

Elizabeth's attentions to Miss Bennet were likely more helpful than those towards her father, but you cannot blame her for caring. She is not well suited to inaction."

Miss Bingley laughed. "Yes, one might mistake her spirit for that of an officer, not a lady. Perhaps why that is so fond of the militia, despite whatever warnings those better informed might give her." She paused, and Elizabeth could not help but feel that she was trying to bait Mr. Darcy into explaining his relationship with Mr. Wickham. Despite her anger at being discussed in such a way, Elizabeth smiled when the man stayed quiet.

Evidently giving up, Miss Bingley continued, "Well, I am sure it is a spirit her husband will soon quash. Can you imagine the pair they shall make! I nearly died suppressing my laughter at such a thought!"

"It is not a matter of ours," Mr. Darcy snapped, voice tight. Somewhat calmer, he continued, "We shall be gone as soon as Mr. Bennet recovers enough to return home. I agree with you that it is wise to separate Bingley from Miss Bennet. He will soon enough find distraction in London with a lady far more worthy of him, and one can only hope with a less grasping mother. She will be nothing to him soon, and we will all be better for it."

Miss Bingley's burst of laughter covered Elizabeth's gasp. Gritting her teeth, the latter hurried away as quietly as she could. Well! No need to wonder what either party thought of her and her family, as if she had cared in any case. But Jane, oh, poor Jane! Were Darcy and Miss Bingley so concerned with status that they cared nothing for matters of the heart? They were quite suited for each other, and Elizabeth hoped with all her heart that they would make each other miserable for the rest of their well-connected, wealthy lives.

Elizabeth had to walk the length of the hallway twice before she calmed down enough to face the nurse and her father with some degree of composure. Reading to him calmed her temporarily, but it also made her pointedly aware of the fact that her father was unable to read for himself—indeed, may never be able to read again. That fear, on top of Jane's pending misery and the undecided problem of Mr. Collins, churned through Elizabeth's mind as she read. Despite her best efforts to focus only on the paper, she made it only half an hour before the exercise became unbearable. Excusing herself to Mrs. Chrisley, Elizabeth left quietly, deliberately making her way towards a lesser-used exit.

Her hand was on the doorknob when Mr. Darcy's voice stopped her. "Miss Elizabeth! You are leaving?"

She turned slowly, cursing her bad timing and schooling her features into a pleasant, if vague, expression. "I am, sir."

"How is your father?" he asked with more interest than she had expected. Of course, she realized a moment later, his motive for asking must be his desire to leave Netherfield as soon as possible.

"His condition is unchanged, at least as far as I could perceive," Elizabeth answered, attempting to keep her voice steady. "You will likely hear of any improvement or—" she stopped, unable to voice the alternative. "That is, I daresay you will be informed of whatever news there is before I am. Good day, Mr. Darcy."

"Wait," he said, and Elizabeth turned back once again. "You do not mean to walk home, Miss Elizabeth, surely? You are distressed, and cannot be expected to think clearly in such a state. I shall call a carriage."

The comment made Elizabeth acutely aware of several things. She had slept for only a few hours, eaten nothing since the previous evening, and was currently standing in a house of people who at best tolerated herself and her family. The last twelve hours had been some of the most trying in her life. In short, she *was* distressed, and the last thing she wanted was for Mr. Darcy to know it.

"I am not in need of a carriage, sir," she replied curtly. "I did not visit this morning with the intent of causing inconvenience to anyone in the household, and I am perfectly capable of returning home under my own power. Good day."

Not waiting for an answer, she opened the door and pulled it firmly closed behind her, cutting off Darcy's objections. He opened the door behind her again, but Elizabeth did not turn. Squaring her shoulders, she walked purposefully down the path towards the main drive. What did it matter if Mr. Darcy thought her actions were *unsuitable for a lady*? He would soon be gone anyhow, back to his precious sister and their elite social circles. Elizabeth had been enjoying her walks for long before the Netherfield party came to the neighborhood, and she would continue to do so long after they left.

If only she didn't feel like crying!

Chapter Four

"Oh, Lizzy, *there* you are!" Mrs. Bennet exclaimed before Elizabeth had even made it through the doorway of Longbourn's sitting room. "What were you thinking, to disappear this morning of all times? Troublesome, ungrateful child. Have you no sympathy for my poor nerves?"

Elizabeth took a deep breath. She'd been expecting this, had in fact been preparing for the confrontation since she left Netherfield. The foresight meant she had taken a longer path around Longbourn and entered through the kitchen door, taking advantage of Mrs. Hill's kindness to eat a hurried late breakfast before making her way upstairs. No amount of strategic planning would allay Mrs. Bennet indefinitely, though, and so Elizabeth squared her shoulders and faced her mother. At least Mr. Collins was not currently in the room

"I have come from Netherfield," she said simply, crossing the room to stand at a window. "I was most anxious to see if Papa had improved."

"Netherfield!" Mrs. Bennet cried. "On foot? There and back? What they must think of you, Lizzy! And you ought not have gone in any case. Jane, Jane should have gone, and taken the carriage. You have ruined all of my plans!"

Elizabeth bit back a retort that Mrs. Bennet had not always been so keen for Jane to take the carriage to Netherfield, but of course *that* scheme had played out perfectly in Mrs. Bennet's eyes. Arriving on horseback soaked to the bone was the reason Jane had fallen ill and been forced to stay at Netherfield in the first place.

"How is my father?" Jane asked, leaning forward and studying Elizabeth with concern. "Has his condition improved?"

"Not noticeably," Elizabeth replied, "but he is comfortably situated, and I found the nurse to be both intelligent and kind. He will be well cared-for."

"Of course he will!" Mrs. Bennet said. "What could he want in a house like that? Oh Jane, if only Mr. Bingley had been able to speak to your father last night."

"It would have been a good deal more romantic than Lizzy's proposal, I am sure," Kitty said, giggling.

"At least Lizzy is assured of a roof over her head," Mrs. Bennet retorted. "I shudder to think would become of us had Mr. Collins not spoken. I shan't even imagine it, for it would tear me to pieces, I am sure! But Lizzy dear, you must not lose his interest! Nothing can be certain until Mr. Bennet gives his agreement. There shall be no more walks like this morning's, of that you may be sure! Mr. Collins was most disappointed to not see you at breakfast."

"You forget, Mama, I have not given my acceptance," Elizabeth replied as calmly as she could. "As you say, nothing can be decided until Papa awakes."

"Lizzy, you must not say such things! Image, if Mr. Collins was to hear, what he would think! Oh, to see a daughter married!"

"It will be strange to see Lizzy take your place," Mary said solemnly, looking up from the pianoforte long enough to cast her gaze around the room.

"Hush, Mary," Mrs. Bennet said. "It will be better than living to see a stranger in my home, and I am sure we will manage."

Mary shrugged and turned back to her instrument.

"Well, I think it is a shame that Mr. Wickham wasn't at the ball to save Lizzy from such an odious man!" Lydia declared. "You won't mind if I steal him from you now, Lizzy, will you? At least one of us should marry someone fun!"

"Hold your tongue, Lydia," Elizabeth said. "Mr. Wickham is hardly in a position to be marrying either of us at the moment, and I certainly never expected an offer from him. Besides, he'll be long gone by the time you are old enough to marry."

"I'm fifteen!" Lydia protested. "I'm old enough to marry *now*, aren't I, Mama? Just because you've waited until you're halfway to being on the shelf doesn't mean I have to!" She gave a cruel smile. "You ought to be glad Mr. Collins proposed— otherwise you'd have ended up like old Charlotte Lucas for sure!"

"Lydia!" Jane and Elizabeth spoke together, and even Jane's usually placid face showed her shock at the comment.

Lydia tossed her head, unabashed. "Well, it's true. And just you wait, I'll marry before either of you—even if Lizzy already does have a fiancé! It will be a lark!"

Jane and Elizabeth met each other's eyes from across the room. They had often tried to check Lydia's behavior, but since Mr. Bennet scarcely bothered to pay attention to his younger daughters and Mrs. Bennet indulged Lydia's every wish, their reprimands had fallen on deaf ears. Now Lydia was out in society as a young lady, but with the mindset of a spoiled little girl. Somehow, she needed to learn that actions had consequences, but Elizabeth had no idea how such a lesson was to be taught.

At that moment, Mr. Collins entered the sitting room and, after greeting the room as a whole, made directly for Elizabeth. Knowing better than to contemplate escape, Elizabeth collected her sewing and settled herself in a comfortable chair.

"I am most glad to see you returned home, Miss Elizabeth," Mr. Collins said, taking the chair across from her.

She opened her mouth to respond, but he did not stop. "I can only assume you went to see to your father's comfort, an admirable reason and one I shall be happy to have in my future wife. Of course, I would have been happy to accompany you, and in the future I must beseech you to notify me before you depart, but do not fear that I shall deny you any such visits, for I am sure your delicate female nature is greatly disturbed by the turn of events and it is my intent to shield you from as much of this unpleasantness as I may. Why, only the other day my most esteemed patroness, the Lady Catherine de Bourgh, was saying to me—"

Elizabeth quit listening. She detested sewing, had managed to choose a chair with a horrid view, and could not think of a single thing to say to Mr. Collins that was both positive and honest. The only saving grace about the situation was that Mr. Collins did not seem to need any input from her to be perfectly happy with the conversation, leaving her mind free to wander. Stifling a sigh, Elizabeth forced her attention to the sewing in her lap. Surely, surely it couldn't be long before her father awoke—could it?

&

No news came from Netherfield that afternoon, or the following day. The third morning passed in similar silence, and by noon Elizabeth was contemplating undertaking the three-mile walk again just to hear if there was any update on her father's condition.

Like the day before, she had risen much earlier than most of her family, but the morning had still been far from peaceful. Elizabeth, knowing better than to push her luck by returning to Netherfield, took her morning walk in the gardens behind the house.

The previous day's clear weather seemed to have fled, leaving in its place grey skies and a bitter wind. It fit her state of mind quite well, Elizabeth mused as she made yet another circuit of the garden.

What in the world was she going to do? Refuse Mr. Collins and the family would have nowhere to go if—if things did not go well at Netherfield. Accept Mr. Collins, and her life would become a certain trial. Elizabeth had watched her parents for long enough to know how miserable she and Mr. Collins would be, for no felicity could exist between a couple where respect did not reside as well.

Nor did Elizabeth expect respect to grow with time. Mr. Collins would not appreciate a wife who challenged him; Elizabeth knew her own mind well enough to be certain she could never respect a man who expected her to be little more than a silent housekeeper. She would be hard pressed to put on a convincing display of respect and duty before society or any children they may have.

And children! The very thought of sharing a marriage bed with Mr. Collins turned her stomach in ways she had never felt before. As a maiden, Elizabeth knew her comprehension of the physical part of marriage was limited, but she had spent enough time around the farm animals at Longbourn to have a base understanding. She couldn't bear to think of kissing the man, let alone whatever came next.

Elizabeth continued to pace, each lap of the garden only increasing her agitation. She must, *must* accept his suit if the unthinkable happened. Even if every bone in her body cried out against the idea, what other solution existed? Surely, he could not be so bad on better acquaintance. Surely, she could find some way to make everything work out. Surely….

Oh, what am I going to do? Shaking her head, Elizabeth walked on.

The thought still ran through her mind as she sat at a window of Longbourn's sitting room that afternoon, sewing neglected in her lap.

"Miss Elizabeth, you seem far more distracted than yesterday," Mr. Collins observed, his direct address catching her attention.

She managed a smile. What would Mr. Collins think if she informed him she had not listened to a word he said the day before? The thought was tempting, if only to see how her would-be husband reacted, but could hardly be expected to produce positive results. Instead, she replied, "I am rather tired, Mr. Collins. I slept poorly, and—"

"Of course, you are still most concerned for your father, and—" he stopped abruptly, mouth hanging open as he stared out the window behind her in shock.

Heart leaping into her throat, for anything that could silence Mr. Collins must be revolutionary, Elizabeth spun to see what had caught his attention. "What is it?"

Her hope of seeing her father, alive and well, was immediately dashed by the sight of an unfamiliar carriage. Drawn by a matched pair of black horses, the carriage was of much finer quality than anything belonging to Longbourn—in fact, it was finer than the Bingleys' carriages as well. Elizabeth's mind went to Mr. Darcy momentarily before noticing the crest on the door. No, whoever rode in the carriage was a stranger, and a rich one at that.

"I don't believe it," Mr. Collins exclaimed, and in a flash of understanding Elizabeth knew who their mystery guest must be.

As the carriage pulled to a stop outside the front door, Elizabeth's guess was confirmed. The door opened to reveal a grand lady that Elizabeth could only imagine was Mr. Darcy's aunt and Mr. Collins' patroness. Lady Catherine de Bourgh had arrived.

Chapter Five

It was hard to determine, Elizabeth thought, if Lady Catherine's arrival had more of an effect on Mr. Collins or Mrs. Bennet. Both leapt to their feet immediately and surveyed the room with wild eyes.

"Oh, good lord," Mrs. Bennet cried. "Girls, quickly now, help me clean up!"

"Straighten that chair!" Mr. Collins demanded, pointing across the room.

"Mary, close the instrument and help!"

"Cousin Lydia, put away that hat!"

"Kitty, *quit coughing*! Oh, my nerves!"

"At least Mama is helping us clean," Elizabeth said in aside to Jane as she tucked a bundle of cloth out of sight and straightened the candlesticks sitting on a table. Jane glanced up from tidying a pile of books and letters and gave her a quick smile in response, but said nothing.

It was just as well, for at that moment voices sounded in the hall outside. Elizabeth dropped onto a sofa next to Mary, both of them sitting up far straighter than they would on a normal afternoon at home. "Smile," Elizabeth whispered to her sister, then bit back a snort of nervous laughter at Mary's half-hearted grimace.

Mrs. Hill opened the sitting room door, but Lady Catherine did not wait for an introduction. She swept into the room several feet before pausing to survey the scene before her with critical eyes. The ladies stood and curtseyed; Mr. Collins made one of his ridiculous bows.

Mr. Collins immediately greeted their visitor in a manner remarkably superfluous even for him. Lady Catherine, apparently used to her clergyman's chatter, acknowledged him only with a slight inclination of her head before making her way farther across the room and taking a seat. Elizabeth returned to her seat slowly, noticing from the corner of her eye that her sisters followed her suit.

"Which one of you is Miss Elizabeth Bennet?" Lady Catherine asked, cutting across Mr. Collins when he paused to draw breath.

"I am," Elizabeth replied with a steadiness she did not feel, sitting up even straighter and raising her chin. So, that was the reason for Lady Catherine's visit. Mr. Collins had likely written to tell her that he was engaged—and probably that Longbourn was soon to be his as well. Well, drat the man, but she did not intend to provide any reason for the lady to disprove of her.

"That lady, I suppose, is your mother."

"She is."

"Lady Catherine, may I present Mrs. Thomas Bennet of Longbourn?" Mr. Collins interjected, and Lady Catherine visibly sniffed. Elizabeth stifled a smile. According to rank, Mr. Collins should have introduced Lady Catherine to her mother, not the other way around. Of course, the rule was sometimes set aside when the introduction was made at the lower ranking person's home, but Elizabeth doubted Lady Catherine would hold with such a notion— unless, perhaps, the lady chanced to meet a duchess at her own estate.

"This," Mr. Collins announced, turning to face the room and bringing his arms up ever so slightly as if he sought to make himself appear larger, "is the Lady Catherine de Bourgh of Rosings Park, my most highly esteemed patroness."

Lady Catherine spared the man a glance before she looked back at Elizabeth. "And these, I suppose, are your sisters."

"My cousins—" Lady Catherine turned to Mr. Collins and silenced him with a look, then returned her haughty gaze to Elizabeth.

Oh, how like Mr. Darcy! Elizabeth thought, taking care to conceal her amusement at the resemblance.

"This is my oldest sister, Jane," she said, "and this is Mary, Catherine, and Lydia." She gestured to each sister in turn, and they inclined their heads as they were acknowledged. Mary still looked rather sullen at the interruption to her pianoforte playing, but at least Lydia had not yet begun to speak of officers, Elizabeth mused.

"You have a very small park here," Lady Catherine observed after a short silence.

"I am sure it seems so to you," Elizabeth replied before Mr. Collins could begin listing all the ways that Longbourn fell short of the Rosings Park, "and likely I would agree if I were used to a home such as the grand estate that Mr. Collins has described, but I must confess that I am fond of our grounds. They are my home, after all, and if only for that reason I shall always look upon them with pleasure."

Lady Catherine appeared taken aback at Elizabeth's statement, and even Mr. Collins seemed to be momentarily speechless.

"My Lizzy has always loved our park," Mrs. Bennet said in a somewhat breathless voice, and

Elizabeth wondered if her mother's nerves were caused by addressing Lady Catherine or the impudence she herself had shown by daring to disagree with that lady. "She is a great walker," Mrs. Bennet added, then fell silent as if fearing she had said too much.

The pause in conversation revealed the sounds of others in the hallway, and all heads swiveled towards the door. It opened to reveal Mrs. Hill, and close behind her were Mr. Bingley and Mr. Darcy.

All the inhabitants immediately rose to greet the new arrivals. Without knowing she did so, Elizabeth leaned forward and looked anxiously from man to man, desperate for any news of her father. Mr. Bingley was oblivious to her silent plea, his eyes going directly to her sister and remaining there, but Mr. Darcy caught her eye.

"Darcy!" Lady Catherine exclaimed. "What are you doing here?"

Mr. Darcy held Elizabeth's gaze for a heartbeat longer and gave a tiny shake of his head before turning his attention to his aunt. The lady had apparently caught the exchange, for her eyebrows snapped together and she glanced in Elizabeth's direction before seeming to dismiss her in favor of her nephew.

Elizabeth fixed a pleasant smile on her face and returned to her seat. No news was good news, she told herself firmly, far better than bad news. No news meant there was still hope. But it was still a struggle to maintain her composure and hide the fears weighing on her heart, and in her focus to appear calm, Elizabeth lost track of the conversation.

"Please, don't let us interrupt you," Mr. Darcy was saying when she managed to turn her focus back to the group.

Elizabeth frowned. Mr. Darcy considering someone other than himself? Then she noticed how he had turned slightly away from his aunt and almost laughed at her discovery. No, Darcy still thought only of himself.

"We were speaking of the park here at Longbourn," Lady Catherine said. "I would hear your opinion on it, Darcy. I find it dreadfully small, but Miss Elizabeth claims such a defect can be excused because it is her home."

Darcy looked sharply at Elizabeth, and she wondered what thoughts were concealed behind his impassive expression and those dark eyes that searched while giving nothing away. "I have seen nothing particularly noteworthy about the park," he said, looking back at his aunt. "However, we must all be partial to those places we love best, and therefore I believe Miss Elizabeth makes a sound point." He turned towards her and the corner of his mouth twitched up into a tiny smile. "I would declare Pemberley to be the most remarkable place in all of England, but I do not pretend to judge without bias."

Caught off guard by his support, Elizabeth still felt her lips curve into an answering smile at his comment. Lady Catherine sniffed. "That is because Pemberley *is* the most beautiful place in England."

"You would hold it above Rosings, then?" Darcy inquired, finally looking away from Elizabeth. "Or the palace gardens, which I have never seen duplicated, or your childhood home at Matlock?"

Another sniff. "The palace gardens lack elegance, and my brother has not kept Matlock as he should." Seeming to remember she was in company, Lady Catherine turned back to Elizabeth. "It is lucky, in your case, that you are happy with your home and do not aspire for a situation out of your reach. It must be a great comfort to know that you are to stay here always. It would break my heart to think of Rosings Park leaving the family, but then, there is no entail on the estate."

"Indeed, I hope to call this my home for some time," Elizabeth replied calmly. "Of course, nothing can be decided until I am able to speak with my father. I would not presume to disregard his thoughts and wishes on the matter." Should her father make a full recovery, Elizabeth thought it likely that he would oppose her marriage to Mr. Collins as strongly as she did. If he did not recover, then she was facing a much different situation—but she did not intent to tie herself to a man and seal her fate while there was still hope for escape.

"What is this?" Lady Catherine asked sharply. "Surely you do not mean to throw away the favor that Mr. Collins has extended to you. Have you no sense, girl?" She turned to Mrs. Bennet. "She is not simple, is she?"

From the corner of her eye, Elizabeth saw Mr. Darcy open his mouth.

"I am not simple," she said firmly before either Mr. Darcy or her mother could reply, "and I am aware of the compliment my cousin has paid me. My intention is only to present an accurate description of where matters stand. Mr. Collins has proposed, but I have not accepted his hand. You must understand, Lady Catherine, as a fellow female, that my fate is not entirely my own to decide. I have not yet reached my majority, and I do not mean to do my father the injustice of forming an understanding with a man— any man—without his approval." She paused. "You have a daughter, I understand. Surely you would not wish her to marry against your wishes."

Lady Catherine's head snapped back. "That is impossible. Anne's fate has long been decided. She is engaged to Darcy and has been her entire life. It was the favorite wish of his mother as well as hers.

We planned the union while they were in their cradles." She seemed poised to continue, but instead cut Darcy a look Elizabeth found indecipherable and fell silent.

"Then I image you would indeed be distressed should she decide to marry elsewhere," Elizabeth remarked. "That is my plight, your ladyship, and I am grateful to think you can view it with sympathy."

The lady's expression turned frosty. "There was a small but pleasant sort of wildness to one side of the house," she said in a deadly calm voice. "I am in need of exercise after my journey this morning. If you would accompany me, Miss Elizabeth? No, Mr. Collins, you are to stay here!" she added when the man would have leapt to his feet to join them.

"Yes, Lizzy, go and show her ladyship the walks," Mrs. Bennet said at once. "I am sure she will be pleased with the hermitage."

Elizabeth rose and smoothed her skirts. "If you will excuse me for a moment, madam, I will fetch my pelisse." She exited the room quickly and wasted no time retrieving the garment from her room. It was warm for November, but Lady Catherine did not seem to be the type of person who would consider her companion's comfort, and the last thing Elizabeth wanted was to appear at any sort of a disadvantage.

Returning downstairs, Elizabeth paused before the final corner to steady herself. She could only assume

Lady Catherine had something to say that she did not want the entire room to hear, and Elizabeth's impression of the lady from the last half-hour was that she did not conceal much. Peeking into a mirror, Elizabeth checked that her hair was in place and then shook her head at her reflection. She would find out soon the reason for Lady Catherine's walk—like it or not.

Giving her reflection a final look, Elizabeth squared her shoulders and rounded the corner to with a smile for her most undesired guest.

Chapter Six

Lady Catherine stopped three times on the way out of the house. The first two times were to open doors, first to the dining room and then to the drawing room, and survey each silently for a moment before moving on. After both had been inspected, she pronounced them decent-looking rooms, and Elizabeth tried to ignore the voice in her mind that instantly tacked the words *for a family like yours* onto the end of the sentence.

The third time Lady Catherine stopped was at the front door. She stood there impatiently for a moment before Elizabeth realized that the lady was waiting for someone else to open the door. Biting back a rude comment—she hadn't had trouble opening doors to snoop—Elizabeth held the door open for her guest and closed it behind them.

Her carriage remained just outside the door, and through the window Elizabeth saw that a companion—likely Lady Catherine's lady's maid—

was waiting inside. It occurred to her that Mr. Darcy must have seen the carriage on his way in, and she wondered what he had thought at finding his aunt at Longbourn.

The pair proceeded in silence along the path leading to the area that Lady Catherine had referenced, the silence lasting until they stood in the middle of a small copse of trees.

"Well," Lady Catherine began, "I will not insult you by explaining why I asked you to accompany me out here. Doubtless your conscience has made you well aware of the reason."

Elizabeth saw the trick immediately. She could either admit to not knowing, a mere ten minutes after Lady Catherine had questioned her mental capabilities, or she could pretend to know the reason and essentially confess her guilt to whatever Lady Catherine might accuse her.

Elizabeth chose the former. "I have no idea to what I owe this honor. I would be most grateful if your ladyship would explain."

"Deceitful girl!" Lady Catherine exclaimed. "I see through your ruse, your plan! Well, hear me when I say you will not succeed! My nephew will not be swayed by you, whatever feminine wiles you have employed to entrap him! Have you not heard me say he is destined for his cousin!"

Now Elizabeth was truly confused. She had assumed that Lady Catherine wanted to talk to her about what would be expected from a wife of the lady's clergyman. She had even considered that a threat or two might be issued. But this? This was completely unexpected insanity.

"I beg your pardon," Elizabeth began, still managing to maintain her calm manner, although it took considerably more effort than before. What she would give to have Jane's temperament at the moment! "I think your ladyship has made a mistake in my intentions. In fact, I am sure of it."

Lady Catherine opened her mouth angrily, but Elizabeth cut across her. "I have used no feminine wiles on Mr. Darcy, and I am certain he would not respond to them if I were to attempt such a tactic. Your nephew is not a man to be easily swayed by the wishes of others. In any case, I do not desire to entrap him, and in fact I had never so much as considered a marriage between Mr. Darcy and myself before you introduced the matter."

"Miss Bennet," Lady Catherine said, "I will not be trifled with. Your pretty lies might be accepted in the company you are accustomed to, but they will not work on *me*. I saw the look you gave my nephew when he entered, and what is more I saw him respond to you! So you see, you can hide nothing from me! I will not be fooled by a country chit. Mr. Collins mentioned that you were dancing with my nephew when your father fell, how you pretended to faint and made him catch you. He mentioned it to thank me for my nephew's goodness of heart, but I knew at once what was afoot. You think to keep Mr. Collins in your power until your father recovers, after which you will cast him off in favor of Mr. Darcy!"

"I think no such thing!" Elizabeth exclaimed, her control over her temper rapidly deteriorating. Two days of constant stress and little sleep were hardly beneficial when one was attempting to remain calm under false accusations.

"Then you mean to have Mr. Darcy in any case?" Lady Catherine queried. "I tell you, I will not allow it! Mr. Darcy is engaged to *my* daughter. Now what have you to say?"

"If that is the case, then you do him a disservice by supposing he could be swayed in his attentions," Elizabeth snapped. "For myself, I do not, and never have, intended to marry Mr. Darcy."

Quick as a snake, Lady Catherine asked, "And will you promise me that you never shall?"

"No!" Elizabeth burst out, furious. "I will make no promises to someone so wholly unconnected to me on what I consider to be a private matter. Additionally, Lady Catherine, I would add that you seem quite concerned with the matter despite your declaration that Mr. Darcy shall marry Miss de Bourgh."

"Is this the insubordination I am to expect from the wife of my clergyman? You owe me a great deal, Miss Bennet! Mr. Collins never would have thought to choose one of his cousins for a wife if I had not commanded he look here first! I sent him here to find a bride with the intention of taking such a young lady under my wing and providing guidance far greater than any you could hope to find in your simple country home.

"Mr. Collins has told me all about your family's behavior—the most pertinent of which is you and your sister throwing yourselves at any present men of fortune with ample encouragement from your mother—your many unmarried sisters with no prospects, your connections in *trade*, and I thought to elevate you as best I could—though obviously you are not meant for the highest circles—by providing an example you can truly look up to. All this could have been yours. It still could, if you cast away your impudence and promise to temper your behavior from here on. Your family will be nothing without my favor. Will you still deny me the assurances I seek?"

The blood pounded in Elizabeth's ears like a drum. Never before had she been so angry. *So this is why men call each other out,* she thought distantly. *This is why they break the law and challenge each other to duels.*

"I shall never give you your assurances," Elizabeth said. Her voice sounded strange in her ears, as if someone else spoke from far away. "You have now insulted myself and those I hold dear in every conceivable way, and can have nothing else to say. I bid you good day, your ladyship."

She faced Lady Catherine and sank into a low curtsey, the kind used only at court, but kept her face upturned and her eyes fixed directly on the other lady's. Perhaps it would have been more suitable to walk away, Elizabeth thought, but then she wouldn't have had the pleasure of watching Lady Catherine's eyes widen infinitesimally as she held her position for long moments without a single wobble. She would have missed seeing the lady turn away first. And as Lady Catherine stormed back towards the house, Elizabeth considered that treating the woman almost as if she were royalty may have been the most effective way of making her realize just how little control she truly held.

§

Elizabeth was still in the garden when Lady Catherine's carriage rolled away in a great cloud of dust several minutes later. She could imagine her mother's distress, the protestations that Elizabeth was under a great deal of stress, surely her ladyship could understand, surely? She wondered if Lady Catherine had bothered to answer Mrs. Bennet, or if she had simply taken her leave of Mr. Darcy and Mr. Collins and left. Perhaps Jane would come find her soon and tell her what had happened—but no, Jane had Mr. Bingley to think of.

The air rushed out of Elizabeth's lungs and she sat down hard on a cold stone bench. Had Lady Catherine simply left without speaking, or had she declared her opinion of Elizabeth to the whole room? It would have been clear to everyone, when the ladies did not return together, that something was wrong. Here was yet another strike against the Bennet family, and no matter how besotted Mr. Bingley was with Jane, he could not have failed to miss this one. If Lady Catherine held any sway with her nephew, Mr. Darcy might very well use the day's events to convince Mr. Bingley that Jane was not worth the trouble.

After so long of worrying that her younger sisters' behavior would ruin Jane's chances for happiness, Elizabeth was forced to consider that her own rash words might be the force that finally separated the couple. It was a bitter thought, and hot tears formed in Elizabeth's eyes as fear and regret mixed with her residual anger. Oh, why hadn't she managed to hold her tongue!

"Why, Miss Elizabeth, I did not expect to find you pining for me," a voice said from several feet in front of her. "I hurried back as quickly as I could manage."

Elizabeth jumped, attempting to wipe her eyes as she sat up. Mr. Wickham's smiling face greeted her, although his expression quickly turned to concern as he took in her countenance.

"Mr. Wickham," she said, trying to hide the confusion in her voice. "I did not expect to see you. You startled me."

"Were you expecting your beloved fiancé?" he asked, then laughed when she gave him a sharp, startled look. Had he overheard her conversation with Lady Catherine? "The soldiers told me I missed a great deal at the Netherfield ball," Mr. Wickham continued, and Elizabeth relaxed a little. "I hear Mr. Collins made quite a romantic proposal."

His lighthearted manner, coming after two days of fear and arguments, felt like a balm to Elizabeth. "It was the type of offer any young lady would dream of receiving," she said. The tone fell flat of her usual teasing manner, but she managed a small smile—and then burst out laughing as the ridiculousness of Mr. Collins' proposal washed over her.

"In that case, I had better make a study of your cousin while I have the chance," Mr. Wickham said. "My idea of what a young lady desires in a man is quite different indeed. For example," he flashed her a brilliant smile and bowed over her hand. "You seem distraught, young lady. Allow me to be your knight in shining armor and banish whatever dragons attempt to disturb you. All I ask in return is that you join me for a stroll and give me the great gift of your company for an afternoon."

Elizabeth smiled at him but stood without accepting his hand. "I would love to walk with you, but I cannot. It would not be proper to walk alone, and I am sure someone will be coming to look for me soon."

Mr. Wickham's eyes drifted over her shoulder to look at the house, and Elizabeth resisted the urge to look as well. He returned his gaze to her and some of the playfulness seemed to have disappeared. "Are you truly going to marry your cousin?"

She looked away. "I do not know yet." After the scene with Lady Catherine, Elizabeth had even more doubts that she and Mr. Collins would have even a chance at a happy marriage, but she would not say that aloud until she was sure of her own mind. Not to anyone other than Jane, at least.

"There are other men who would be happy to marry you—and your sisters," Mr. Wickham continued. He smiled again, playfulness back in full force. "Remember that. I would be more than willing to hire a carriage for Gretna Green."

Elizabeth's eyes widened in shock and she took a half-step back, but Mr. Wickham was already backing away and bowing in farewell. "Your would-be fiancé approaches, my fair lady. Remember what

I said, if you need a knight in shining armor." Taking another two steps away, he called back over his shoulder in a voice meant to carry, "Pass my regards on to the other ladies of the house. I will call again at a better time."

Elizabeth took a steadying breath and tried to put Mr. Wickham's inappropriate comments out of her mind. Perhaps her cousin would be reasonable. Perhaps she could convince him that they would never be happy together, and suggest that Mary would make a fine wife for a clergyman. Perhaps he would be as relieved as she.

She turned to face the approaching man and all hopeful thoughts fled her mind. Mr. Collins was almost upon her, and the look on his face was nothing short of thunderous.

Chapter Seven

Mr. Collins came to a halt directly in front of Elizabeth. His face was bright red, which stood out brilliantly next to his white cravat, and his chest heaved as if he had just finished running.

"Miss Elizabeth, never in my life have I been so mortified," he began in solemn tones, then flicked his eyes to Mr. Wickham's retreating form. The latter's presence seemed to confuse him, as if he had planned a great speech and now didn't know quite how to proceed. "And who in the world is that man?"

"That is one of the officers stationed in Meryton," Elizabeth replied. "He was away during the Netherfield ball and was just informed of Mr. Bennet's condition. He came to call on the family, but I have informed him that now is not the most, ah, ideal time."

Mr. Collins scowled. "And he has done so before?"

"Yes, several times."

"I find it quite improper that he should speak to you alone. He should have continued to the house."

"And ignored me completely?" Elizabeth asked in some astonishment. "I do not make a habit of seeking out young men for private interludes, and in any other chance meeting would have taken him to the house at once, but you must see that exchanging *no* words would have been equally improper. Besides, Mr. Collins, allow me to point out that you are speaking to me alone at this very moment."

"That is a completely different matter. A man may, following the happy event in which a lady accepts his hand, expect that the rules of society give way to allow him—"

"Mr. Collins, I do not mean to be rude, but I have not accepted your hand. I believe I have made myself clear on this matter, but let me repeat: we are not engaged."

Her cousin's doughy face took on a self-satisfied look. "Dear Cousin Elizabeth, I pride myself on understanding members of the fairer sex well enough to determine what is going on here, and your modesty and adherence to propriety both add to your overall qualities and allure. You would have, in fact, fallen in my esteem should you not have shown such an unwillingness to spend time in private with myself, and I am overjoyed to confirm this aspect of your near perfection. Allow me, madam, to put you at ease and assure you that, unlike that other young man, gentleman though he surely is, I have your mother's express permission to attend to you in such an individual manner. In fact, she was most encouraging of my intentions."

He paused, and his lofty expression turned to a scowl. "I am currently most displeased with you, Miss Elizabeth, but I am an agreeable, forgivable sort of man, and I therefore shall condescend to view your actions in light of the utmost distress the last several days has no doubt bestowed upon you. Similar behavior in the future shall be met with much less leniency, but I believe you to be a young woman who will rise to the occasion, and so I will continue with my original intent."

Elizabeth turned to stare at him in astonishment, and once again his face morphed back into its customary self-righteous countenance. She thought to hide her expression, but such an act was not required—Mr. Collins turned his entire body slightly away and looked up at a nearby tree, clasping his hands in front of him.

"You must be certain of that intent; even without the ill-fated events of the Netherfield ball, my attentions to your person can surely have been too direct to miss interpret. You are the lifelong companion, the dearest partner in domestic felicity, for which I have been searching."

63

Elizabeth drew breath to speak, but he continued speaking across her.

"I came to Hertfordshire to see the house I am one day to inherit, true, but my main intent of visiting Longbourn was to find a wife." A frown returned to his face. "Excepting of this morning's events, I have determined quite to my satisfaction that you will fit all of my needs impeccably, and indeed I daresay that you will make me the happiest of all men. I am sure you will soon come to regret your actions towards my most esteemed patroness, whatever they were, but do not fret, my dear cousin, for in our affection I do not doubt that we will soon cease to think of it altogether."

Mr. Collins' features were once again arranged in the pompous mask Elizabeth had come to associate with him—he seemed to have talked himself out of any possible deterrents to his affection for her, and she could hardly keep herself from gaping in outright horror. His condescending ways aside, she could only imagine the evils that would come from tying herself to a man set on believing delusions.

But he was not finished. "Of course, before I am lost in the tide of my emotions, I ought to list the reasons that I have decided to marry. I am sure you will be in agreement in this as in all matters of our life together. First, that I think it a right thing for every clergyman in easy circumstances like myself to set the example of matrimony in his parish. Secondly, that I am convinced it will add very greatly to my happiness.

"Thirdly, which perhaps I ought to have mentioned earlier, it is the particular advice and recommendation of the very noble lady whom you recently met. Twice has she condescended to give me her opinion on this subject; and it was but the very Saturday night before I left Hunsford that she told me directly that I *must* marry, and marry a gentlewoman at that. She recommended an active, useful sort of woman, brought up well but not too high, and accustomed to living on a smaller income. I am sure that she will be most forgiving of your lapse of propriety and sense, and your wit and vivacity I think must be acceptable to her, especially when tempered with the silence and respect which her rank will inevitably excite when you are in a stable state of mind."

Oh, I doubt that very much, Elizabeth thought. She was well enough aware of her own behavior and temperament to know that her father's situation and the stress of the last few days had made her less patient and more irritable in her dealings with others. She did not delude herself, though, that any situation could bring about true respect for Catherine de Bourgh while the lady treated her in the manner she had just witnessed. Doubtful that Mr. Collins would listen to her but determined to try even so, Elizabeth drew breath to speak.

"Of course," he went on, cutting over her attempted response once again, "it remains to be told why my views were directed to Longbourn instead of my own neighborhood, where I assure you there are many amiable young women. In light of recent events, I am sure you understand all too well what fate would befall you, your mother, and your sisters in the event of your father's death, were not one of you married to his successor.

"Since this title falls to me, and because I flatter myself that I am neither blind to your situation nor heartless, I could not satisfy myself without resolving to choose a wife from among your family, so that you feel this loss as little as possible. This has been my motive, my fair cousin, and I flatter myself it will not sink me in your esteem. And now nothing remains for me but to assure you in the most animated language of the violence of my affection."

Elizabeth had heard enough and could no longer stay silent. After Lady Catherine's speech, little of what Mr. Collins said had caught her by surprise, but it was demeaning and galling none the less. When Mr. Collins at last stopped for breath, she began in a much more forceful manner than before, "Mr. Collins, I must beg you to hear me out."

His eyebrows snapped together, and Elizabeth realized that her input was not expected, nor was it wanted. She was nothing more than a prop, a woman to be brought home for display because Lady

Catherine demanded it and—perhaps, although Elizabeth was not sure she believed her cousin—to assuage his guilt at inheriting Longbourn. Clenching one hand into a fist in the folds of her skirt, Elizabeth reined in her temper once again. It would not do to give in to either anger or tears; likely Mr. Collins would dismiss anything said in such a way. She would have to be calm.

"Sir, you are too hasty. It is the accepted practice, is it not, for a suitor to allow his intended lady a chance to respond to his advances. I beg that you let me do so now, before you speak farther of a situation that I have not accepted. And while I am quite sensible to the honor you pay me with such a proposal, my conscious will not allow me to do anything other than decline it!"

Mr. Collins gave a lofty wave of his hand, as if dismissing her refusal was no different than brushing off a pesky fly. "I flatter myself that I understand elegant females often reject the addresses of the man whom they secretly mean to accept, when he first applies for their favor, sometimes going so far as to reject it two or three times. I am therefore by no means discouraged by what you have just said, and as I said before, your modesty and sense of propriety do you credit."

She turned on her heel to face him full on. "You do me a grave disservice, sir, by believing me to be one of these *elegant females*, if indeed such ladies do

67

exist! I have never heard of such a thing, and I find the idea entirely reprehensible! To not only risk one's happiness on the chance of being asked a second time, but to also tread on the feelings of a man one hopes to wed is a most shameful sort of insanity. I mean every word I say. I do not intend to marry you, and I will not change my mind no matter how many times you ask me. You could not make me happy, and I am convinced I am the last woman in the world who could bring you marital felicity."

Thinking of her recent encounter with the woman largely responsible for the current situation, Elizabeth added, "I am certain Lady Catherine does not approve of me at all, and from our parting words I believe she would be most unpleased if you were to choose me as wife and mistress of your parsonage. Surely, sir, given the reasons you gave me for marrying, this objection must weigh heavily upon you."

He nodded at her in a patronizing fashion, as if she were a small child who had just grasped the truth of the situation. "You are quite correct, Cousin Elizabeth, in your assumptions. However, given time, I am sure the lady will grow accustomed to you and find your company quite acceptable. You are removed from any truly important persons in this area, and I am sure your behavior will improve remarkably under close exposure and, of course, my own husbandly guidance."

"Mr. Collins, you seem to remain under the delusion that I am to marry you. Please understand me when I say I wish you nothing but the best, and I know my own temperament well enough to assure you that you will not find happiness with me. In making me the offer, you must have satisfied the delicacy of your feelings with regard to my family and I shall expect nothing more from you." She turned away, planning on returning to the house. "I believe we are finished here, sir."

A hand grasped her forearm and tightened to the point where Elizabeth wasn't sure she could pull away.

"Unhand me at once, Mr. Collins," she demanded, swinging back to face him.

He took a step forward. He was not a tall man, but the expression on his face gave him a dangerous look. "You should be grateful I offered for you at all, Cousin Elizabeth. I was half convinced not to, after your disgraceful behavior both this morning to a lady far more important that yourself and the grasping way you clung to Mr. Darcy at the ball. I am a patient man, but I will not be toyed with after a display such as you gave this morning. As my wife, you will need to learn the obedience that your father has been woefully poor at teaching you."

She jerked backwards with little luck. "You are in luck, for I will certainly not be marrying you! You can find a much more *obedient* wife somewhere else."

"You *will* marry me, and you *will* be obedient!" he hissed, drawing back his free arm.

For the first time in the entire exchange, Elizabeth felt fear snake through her body. Then, abruptly, Mr. Collins' eyes widened. Almost in the same instant, Elizabeth was jerked away from her cousin, spun around, and set back down facing the opposite direction. By the time she had caught her balance enough to turn back, she could not see Mr. Collins at all. Instead, she was staring directly at a gentleman's back, his broad shoulders and dark hair filling her field of view. Mr. Darcy had entered the scene.

Chapter Eight

Elizabeth didn't know if she should laugh or cry. It was too much to process. She had entirely forgotten that Mr. Darcy was a guest at Longbourn that morning; had, in fact, forgotten much beyond the desperate desire to make her cousin take her seriously. It all came rushing back as she stood staring at Mr. Darcy's back, rubbing her arm where Mr. Collins had gripped it and gasping for air as she tried desperately to calm down.

It's too much. Lady Catherine, Mr. Wickham, Mr. Collins, Mr. Darcy. It's too much.

Mr. Darcy was talking, but Elizabeth couldn't make out the words. Mr. Collins attempted to interject, his nasally voice somewhat less pompous than usual. Darcy cut him off and took a half step towards the smaller man. Even from behind him, Elizabeth felt his anger. Then Mr. Collins scurried off abruptly in the direction of the house.

Darcy turned on his heel to face her. His usual impassive, haughty mask had disappeared, to be replaced with white-faced rage. She flinched without meaning to but stayed put, staring up at him and pulling her arms in tighter around her middle.

The anger vanished and Darcy frowned in concern. "Forgive me, Miss Elizabeth, if I startled you," he said tightly.

"No, I—" Elizabeth stopped, dropping her gaze. Oh, why had all of her verbosity deserted her? In the last two days, she had become quite different from the laughing, quick-witted, independent Lizzy Bennet that she had always believed herself to be. She had failed to keep control of herself and her situation, let her temper threaten her family's security, and very well may have been the final straw that drove Mr. Bingley away from Jane. And now, to her great embarrassment, she could not even form a complete sentence in front of a man who must think her very simple indeed.

A man who had just intervened at a very embarrassing, very opportune moment. Elizabeth's mind wandered to what could have happened if Mr. Darcy had not come upon them when he did, and realized that there was one thing she could say— should say—without needing to think.

"Thank you, sir."

Some of the anger returned to his face, but he gave a slight bow. "I was concerned when my aunt returned without you. She is not known for her kindness, even to those she does not consider below her. I am well aware of your fondness for roaming the countryside, and thought you may have decided to do so after your conversation. Mr. Collins saw her out and said he would take care of the matter, but when he failed to return as well, I made up my mind to investigate. If a member of my family caused some misfortune to befall you, I find myself duty-bound to put the matter to rights."

The words were not unkind, and on a different day Elizabeth might have laughed off the conceited manner in which they were delivered. In her present state, though, she heard only two things—that she was inferior to Lady Catherine and most likely to Mr. Darcy himself as well, and that he thought himself better suited to take care of her than she could manage herself.

"Well, as you can see, I did not go running off, and thanks to your timing I am well. You have done more than your duty and do not need to worry in regard to me." She took a deep breath and squared her shoulders. "If you will excuse me, I ought to return to the house. The others will be concerned as to my whereabouts as well." Or at least Jane would be concerned. Elizabeth doubted the rest of her sisters would care, and her mother would care only about her response to Mr. Collins.

Not waiting for Mr. Darcy's response, Elizabeth hurried back to the house. She encountered Mrs. Hill in the entryway and, giving her standard excuse of a headache, managed to escape upstairs to her room for the remainder of the day.

&

Elizabeth woke the next morning with the unfamiliar feeling of not knowing what she should do. After a night's sleep, fitful though it had been, she no longer found her circumstances overwhelming. They were far from ideal, however, and even her characteristic cheerfulness failed to overcome the dread that curled in her stomach. She could not marry Mr. Collins; she felt no regret for her response to his proposal. But as the days passed, it had become harder to believe in her father's full recovery. Supposing the worst happened, Elizabeth did not know what she, her sisters, and her mother would do—or even what options were truly available to them. As she lay in bed in the early morning light, sleeping next to Jane in the room they had shared for their entire life, the uncertainly of the future terrified her.

That would not do, she decided firmly. She had spent a lifetime watching her mother give in to her fears and doubts with nothing to show for it but an unhappy marriage and poorly managed children. It was a fate Elizabeth had long ago decided she would never allow for herself.

74

So she slid out from beneath the warm covers, smiling as Jane rolled over and pulled the blankets closer around herself. There was still hope for her father, she thought as she dressed quietly and put her hair up in a simple fashion she could manage well on her own. He could live for years still, and while he lived Mr. Collins remained largely powerless over the rest of the household. Elizabeth put the final pins in her hair and examined herself in the small mirror. She raised her chin and forced a smile. Her father had missed hearing the news the last two days. She would not make him forego the pleasure for a third day.

However, it was a cautious Elizabeth who exited Longbourn several minutes later. The previous day had introduced hitherto unknown concerns that she was not soon to forget. Only after considering the fact that both Mr. Collins and Mr. Wickham preferred to sleep late did she set out in earnest.

The walk to Netherfield passed without incident, helped along by the ride she caught from Sir Lucas as far as Meryton. When she expressed the sentiment that Mr. Collins was suffering from the lack of male companionship, he even volunteered to stop at Longbourn on his way home and invite the clergyman to dine with his family that evening. Her mother might bemoan the loss of a chance to force her second daughter into marriage with Mr. Collins, but the rest of the family would certainly welcome the reprieve.

By the time Elizabeth reached Netherfield, her mood had improved significantly, and she was able to look at the surrounding world with her usual optimistic view. She endured a very brief interview with Miss Bingley and Mrs. Hurst, both of whom looked as excited to see her as she was to encounter them, then hurried up the stairs to the small room where her father lay.

Mrs. Chrisley greeted her warmly, and Elizabeth could not help but wonder if anyone in the household had bothered to spend time with her father or his nurse since she had visited last. After a few minutes of small talk that confirmed both her father's lack of progress and the absence of visitors, Elizabeth settled next to him to read.

She was in the middle of an article on the recent Luddite uprisings in the north when she happened to glance up at her father, an automatic response ingrained from years of reading together and talking over the most interesting parts. Still thinking of the article, it took her a moment to realize that Mr. Bennet's eyes were open.

Elizabeth gasped and jumped up, the paper falling to the floor at her feet. "Papa!" she exclaimed, a frantic joy bubbling up inside of her. "Papa, you're awake!"

Mrs. Chrisley bustled over, her dark eyes sharp on Mr. Bennet's face. Just as she reached his side, his eyes drifted closed again, face resuming the same look it had held since he collapsed at the ball.

Elizabeth caught up his limp hand and held onto it tightly. "Papa, can you hear me? Do you need anything? Papa, please wake up!" She looked up at Mrs. Chrisley, eyes frantically searching the nurse's face as if she hoped to find answers there, but unable to put her questions into coherent sentences.

The nurse gave her a reassuring smile and turned her attention back to Mr. Bennet. She placed a hand on his face and lifted one of his eyelids, then the other, before looking up at Elizabeth again.

By this time, Elizabeth had unraveled her thoughts and found her voice. "He opened his eyes, I know he did. Was he truly awake? Will he wake up again?"

"He did open his eyes," Mrs. Chrisley agreed. "I saw that as well. As for your questions, I am not sure. It is hard to tell in cases like these what will happen and what will not. Your father is still in God's hands, and only He knows what the outcome will be." She paused, then continued. "I do not want to give you false hope, but in other instances such as these, those patients who woke up and recovered often exhibited episodes such as we just observed."

Elizabeth closed her eyes for a moment and sent up a fervent prayer that her father was one of those patients. Then she forced herself to take a deep breath and release the white-knuckled grip she still had on her father's hand. "Thank you, Mrs. Chrisley," she managed to say in a controlled, if somewhat shaky, voice. "Whatever the outcome, I thank you for your care of my father and your kind words to me."

The older woman reached out and patted Elizabeth's hand across the bed. "You're welcome, dear. Perhaps you could finish the article you were reading before you leave for the day? If your father is indeed listening, you would not want to leave him in suspense, I am sure."

The suggestion sounded remarkably to Elizabeth like a way of distracting her from her own thoughts, but she acquiesced readily. After reading only a few sentences, however, she stopped and addressed Mrs. Chrisley.

"Will you watch him, and tell me if he opens his eyes again? I fear I will take the rest of the day to finish the article if I look up between every phrase as I am currently inclined to do."

"Of course, dear," the nurse replied easily, turning her chair so she faced Mr. Bennet directly.

Elizabeth took another deep breath, gave her father a final long look, and forced herself to read on.

When the article was finished—in a rather jerky fashion, for she still glanced up at her father's face at least once a paragraph—Mrs. Chrisley rose. "If you will excuse me, I will return soon. Can you stay with your father for several more minutes?"

"Of course," Elizabeth said immediately. "There are plenty more articles for me to read."

But when the nurse had gone, she folded the paper carefully and set it down on the small table next to the bed. "Oh, Papa," she said quietly. "Please wake up soon. There are so many things I want to talk to you about. Mr. Collins and Mama and Lady Catherine—she was awful, Papa, but you could find some humor in the situation, I know you could. And Jane smiles like she always does, but I know she is worried, and Lydia and Kitty will go completely wild if you are not there to offer what guidance and direction you do. Oh Papa, I wish they were not out and could grow out of their foolishness in the privacy of Longbourn.

"Please wake up, Papa. I could not bear it if you do not. Papa, I can't marry him. I can't do it, even if he'd still have me. *I can't.* It would kill me, everything about myself that makes me, *me.* Surely you would understand that, Papa, even if Mama never can. I know she means well, and I worry about my sisters too. Papa, you have to wake up. Come home, Papa, please come home."

Elizabeth stopped, emotions crashing over her like waves, and bent her head. She was exhausted. Giving voice to her worries had tired her far more than the trip from Longbourn to Netherfield had done, and she was left feeling drained. But Mrs. Chrisley would return soon, and Elizabeth would not show the extent of her fears to the nurse, however kind she was. The woman was employed by the Bingleys, and Elizabeth was not naïve enough to think that any secrets she shared would remain as such.

Taking what felt like her thousandth deep breath of the day, Elizabeth smoothed her hands on her gown and straightened, blinking rapidly to clear any hint of tears from her eyes. A hint of movement caught her eye and she jerked, face growing warm even before her mind fully comprehended the situation.

Mr. Darcy was standing in the door, looking as though he had been there for some time.

Chapter Nine

A boiling rage surged up Elizabeth's spine, making the back of her neck tingle. Who did he think he was, this man who intervened and judged with seemingly no regard of the situation? Were others of his acquaintance so enamored by his wealth that they would forgive him his arrogant tendencies? Or was she, a country lady with almost no dowry or status to speak of, simply below the sphere of people he considered worth such niceties as respect or common courtesy?

She remained seated quite deliberately; if Mr. Darcy did not think it appropriate to announce his entrance into a private room, she would not stand and curtesy. Instead, she regarded him steadily for a moment, then turned back to her father. She had not planned to read any more, but rather than sit in silence she picked up the newspaper and opened to a page at random. Settling on the first article she saw—a discussion about the merits of an experimental crop—she began to read aloud.

"Do you often read such articles, or did you choose this for your father's sake?" Mr. Darcy asked after she had made her way through several paragraphs. He moved farther into the room so she could see him clearly from the corner of her eye.

Elizabeth finished the paragraph she was reading before folding the paper on her lap and looking up. "My father and I discuss the contents of the paper— the *entire* paper—each week. He is most interested in this crop, and I have come to feel rather invested in its success, although seeds are still too expensive for us to plant at Longbourn."

Mr. Darcy's brow furrowed as he frowned. "I wouldn't have thought you the type to read the paper cover to cover," he remarked. "My own sister likes to read, but I cannot imagine her sitting down and focusing on a discussion of crops of her own accord."

"I think it is important to keep up with what is happening in the world outside of Hertfordshire," Elizabeth remarked. "So many people live their lives seeing only what is directly in front of them, and yet we are all touched by events larger than ourselves."

"*You* cannot have always been in Hertfordshire, surely," Mr. Darcy said.

Caught by surprise, Elizabeth studied him curiously for a moment before she replied, wondering what true meaning the words carried.

"You are correct," she replied slowly. "I have spent time in London, with my aunt and uncle Gardiner. How much that has expanded my world view or desire to know more than just my home, I cannot say." She paused, thinking about the rest of what he had said. "Did you expect me to read only novels, Mr. Darcy?" Elizabeth found nothing wrong with the new genre and in fact enjoyed reading novels very much, but could not imagine Mr. Darcy would feel the same, or let his precious sister read the books.

Before he could answer, Mrs. Chrisley returned, masking any surprise she felt at Mr. Darcy's presence behind a calm smile. "Good morning, Mr. Darcy," the nurse said.

"Good morning," he responded, with more warmth in his voice than Elizabeth had expected. "How is Mr. Bennet today?"

Mrs. Chrisley glanced at Elizabeth. "Much the same as he has been. We did have an event this morning, did Miss Elizabeth tell you?"

Darcy's eyes cut to Elizabeth, searching her face. "She did not," he said. Still looking at her, he asked, "It was a good event, I hope?"

After several seconds of silence, Elizabeth realized that Mrs. Chrisley would not be responding since Mr. Darcy had addressed her directly. She opened her mouth, then looked away from Mr.

Darcy, uncertain she would be able to keep her calm façade in place well enough to hide any emotion that might show in her eyes. "My father opened his eyes this morning."

"But that is wonderful news," Mr. Darcy said, once again with far more feeling than she could have predicted. In fact, he sounded relieved.

He must be quite anxious to return to London, Elizabeth thought acidly. *I wonder he does not leave now, since it isn't his house.* Aloud, she said, "My father opened his eyes, but he was not truly awake. He did not respond to me, or make any indication that he knew we were present. Mrs. Chrisley has warned me that I am to guard against false hope." *I would have preferred that Mrs. Chrisley not mention this to you at all, Mr. Darcy.*

Mr. Darcy looked away at last, transferring his frown to the nurse. "Surely any change at this point is a positive change, is it not?"

Mrs. Chrisley's eyes flicked to Elizabeth, and the latter wondered if the nurse thought that she, a young lady, could not handle the same information as a man like Mr. Darcy. If so, it would be hypocrisy without a doubt, but nothing Elizabeth had not experienced before. Ladies were to be sheltered and protected where men were informed. The thought made Elizabeth long for her father—awake, healthy, and generous with information—even more.

84

She stood abruptly, feeling unequal to concealing her emotions for any longer. "Excuse me, Mrs. Chrisley, Mr. Darcy. If I am away from home much longer I shall certainly be missed." Elizabeth doubted anything short of accepting Mr. Collins' hand in marriage would diminish her mother's anger, but Mrs. Bennet was not the only person to consider. Caught up in her own struggles, Elizabeth had neglected Jane for the past few days, and her older sister was very likely in more need of a confidant that she would ever let on.

Unsurprisingly, Mr. Darcy rose when Elizabeth did; his base manners were perfect even if his haughty demeanor detracted much from their delivery. "Allow me to accompany you," he said, moving towards the door.

Elizabeth counted to ten silently. It would not do to make a scene in front of the nurse, and if her father could indeed hear the last thing she wanted to do was cause him any stress. Rather than arguing immediately, she took her leave of Mrs. Chrisley and kissed her father's forehead before walking out into the hall, Mr. Darcy following close behind.

They passed several doorways in silence before Elizabeth spoke. "I assure you, Mr. Darcy, I am more than capable of finding my way out of Netherfield and back to Longbourn unaccompanied. You need not trouble yourself."

"You mean to walk the entire way back to Longbourn?" he inquired sharply, tone making it obvious that the statement was an accusation.

She forced herself to keep walking rather than stopping to confront him. "I do, Mr. Darcy."

"Am I to believe this is how you react to the events of yesterday? I did not take you for a fool, Miss Elizabeth."

She saw his point, and had it been suggested by someone else, or in a less disdainful manner, she would have had no choice other than to agree. But Mr. Darcy brought out every contrary impulse she had, and so instead she replied, "There is a stubbornness about me that never can bear to be frightened at the will of others. My courage always rises with every attempt to intimidate me."

"Even when those attempts to intimidate you could result in your bodily harm? Miss Elizabeth, I must insist you allow me to return you home in my carriage."

They had reached Netherfield's front doors, by some miracle avoiding Caroline Bingley's notice, and Mr. Darcy gestured towards the stables as he spoke.

"It is my turn to call you a fool, Mr. Darcy," Elizabeth replied acridly. "Surely you understand what would follow if we were to enter a carriage with no chaperone. I have no desire to enter marriage through a scandal, and I do not doubt that you feel the same. No, sir, I shall return home on my own two feet. Good day."

Elizabeth curtsied and turned on her heel, striding away at a faster pace than was strictly ladylike. For a few heartbeats, she thought she had succeeded. Then Mr. Darcy's footsteps sounded on the gravel of Netherfield's drive as he came after her. "I cannot accept your decision. You may not have been cloistered in the country all your life, but you are still innocent to many of society's evils. If you are determined to walk, then I shall escort you on foot."

"Were we not just discussing my propensity to read the paper and attend to world events, Mr. Darcy?" Elizabeth asked. "You must think me simple indeed if you believe I am still blind to the faults of the society. Besides, how will you return once I have been delivered like a package to my front door?" They had been walking along at a fast clip, but as she asked the last question, Elizabeth stopped and turned her face up to his, squaring her shoulders and setting her jaw.

To her immense surprise, Mr. Darcy took half a step closer so he was looking almost directly down at her, expression a mix of anger and something else, something she couldn't quite read. "If I thought you would wait and not go running off, I would saddle my stallion and take him with us. He will not be worse off for a walk, and I can ride him back once you are safely home."

She quirked an eyebrow, hoping none of her unease showed on her face. "And is your stallion so slow that he could not catch me, even if I did walk on in your absence?"

Mr. Darcy closed his eyes momentarily. "He would find it trivial, Miss Elizabeth, but if my goal is to ensure that no harm comes to you on your way to Longbourn, I run a far greater risk of failing for each minute that you are out of my sight. Mr. Collins is not the only untrustworthy person in the vicinity."

Elizabeth's thoughts went immediately to Mr. Wickham and the great injustice that Mr. Darcy did him. She had not forgotten the previous day's encounter with that gentleman, and while it had unsettled her, there was no question in her mind that Mr. Wickham's company would be preferable to his rival's.

She took a deep breath and tried another approach. "I would ask you frankly, Mr. Darcy, why it is that you are so concerned for my well-being. Despite my cousin's behavior yesterday, there is little chance of harm befalling me, and I am sure you have more important things to do with your time than escort me three miles through the countryside."

The question seemed to catch him off guard. He looked away from her, glancing at their surroundings, and Elizabeth realized that they had come far enough from the house to be entirely alone, with no one from Netherfield in sight and little chance of that changing. She gritted her teeth, cursing the circumstances that had led her into this situation once again.

Mr. Darcy turned back to her abruptly and burst out, "In vain have I struggled. It will not do. My feelings will not be repressed. You must allow me to tell you how ardently I admire and love you."

The declaration caught her utterly off guard, as her previous understanding of his feelings had been so remarkably opposite of his words that she nearly laughed in disbelief. Surely, he must speak in jest!

After a short hesitation, Darcy continued. "I have tried since the moment I laid eyes on you to repress the emotions which you evoked, and find that despite my struggles they have only grown stronger with each encounter. I have considered at length the difference in our circumstances—our status, fortunes, and connections—the gross lack of propriety shown by your family, the response from my family and close acquaintances, and all to no avail. You outweigh them all. I can only beg you now to end my agony and accept my hand in marriage."

Chapter Ten

Elizabeth was nothing short of stunned, but she did not remain so for long. Losing the paralysis that shock had afflicted on her, she glared up and him and realized that he looked, even now, smug! Oh yes, he spoke of warm feelings and the struggle of overcoming his qualms, but the face looking down at her showed only his customary haughty pride.

"That would have been very welcome, I am sure, if I had ever desired such addresses! But I have never desired your good opinion, and you have certainly bestowed it most unwillingly. Do tell me, Mr. Darcy, do you insult all those people of your acquaintance as a way of expressing your warm feelings towards them? If so, I can forgive your standoffish nature around every person you have met here in Hertfordshire, but I should hate to be one of those you hold dear!"

She paused a moment to compose herself before continuing. "If I have led you on in any way, it was most unconsciously done, and I would offer you my apologies did I think you were in need of them. The feelings which, you tell me, have long prevented the acknowledgment of your regard, can have little difficulty in overcoming it after this explanation."

Throughout Elizabeth's speech, Mr. Darcy's face had grown progressively paler. His jaw had clenched, and from the movement of his arms behind his back, Elizabeth suspected his hands were as well. When she finished, he seemed to struggle visibly to maintain his composure, working his jaw several times as if he would speak before finally opening his mouth and giving voice to his thoughts.

"And this is the reply I am to receive! I, who would give up so much for you and your gain, am rejected without even an attempt at civility. I have truly misjudged you if you would reply in such a way without a strong reason."

"Without reason!" Elizabeth exclaimed. "I have every reason in the world to think ill of you. Since the first moment I met you, you have been nothing but arrogant, uncivil, and oftentimes downright rude. You have degraded those I love for no reason other than they were born to a station below you. And now, when you profess supposed love, you do so by telling me that you liked me against your will, against your better reason, and against all that society expects from you. Clearly, sir, you have misjudged me grossly indeed."

She leaned forward. "My own feelings have been fixed against you since they day we met, but even if they were not I would refuse you now. No pretty words, no material rewards could induce me to accept someone who has called my most beloved sister 'nothing' and conspired to ruin her dreams and her happiness, quite possibly forever! What have you to say to that, Mr. Darcy?"

"I will not deny it," he replied smoothly. "My friend counts me as a sound advisor, and I would have done a poor job indeed had I remained silent on the matter. If you will condemn me for protecting a wealthy but naive young man from a fortune hunter, then I gladly accept the blame."

"Yes, because you in all your superiority are privy to those feelings which are often hidden even from the closest of friends. It must feel wonderful to be you, Mr. Darcy, with all of your certainty and never a worry that you are vastly, horribly wrong! You would ruin the happiness of the world around you just to maintain your pride. I now fully understand why Mr. Wickham views you with such spite. It is only a wonder to me that he has any positive attitude towards you left at all."

"You take a great deal of interest in matters which do not concern you," Mr. Darcy hissed.

"Who could help but feel concerned, should they know of his misfortunes?" she fired back.

Darcy's face twisted into she would have called a sneer on a lesser man. "Yes, his great misfortunes. He is the type of man that provokes pity easily, though it has been years since he inspired any feeling of true substance, much less one which he deserved."

"*He* has been attentive and understanding," Elizabeth said. "Had I known how the last day and a half would go, I would have accepted his offer to elope and been better off for it!"

The last statement came out in a rush with no thought on Elizabeth's part other than frustration and overwhelming exhaustion, and the effect on Mr. Darcy was immediate. She had thought him pale before, but at her words he turned nothing short of *white*. "He would not dare," Mr. Darcy whispered, almost more to himself than to her. His eyes closed as if in agony, and for the first time throughout the conversation, Elizabeth felt sorry for the gentleman. It could not be easy to hear the woman you hoped to marry preferred your rival, no matter who was at fault in the rivalry.

The silence stretched on between them, calling Elizabeth's notice to their ragged breathing and the pounding of her heart. Finally, eyes still closed and in a manner devoid of nearly all emotion, Darcy said, "So this is your opinion of me. Had I been aware of your sentiments, I would never have broached the manner and caused such damage to your pride by simply being honest with you." His lips twisted. "I owe you an apology."

Two could play at that game. "Not at all, Mr. Darcy. Your manner saved me from the regret I should have felt, had you behaved in a more gentleman-like manner."

His eyes flew open, but Elizabeth did not wait to hear his reply. Turning smartly on her heel, she walked away, and this time, Mr. Darcy did not follow.

&

Mrs. Bennet and all of her sisters were in the sitting room when Elizabeth returned. Unsurprisingly, Mrs. Bennet confronted her the moment she walked through the door, bemoaning the fact that all of them would have to leave it forever before long when Mr. Collins ungraciously kicked them out into the cold.

"And what we shall do then is beyond me, for we will have little money and nowhere to go, all thanks to your selfishness!" Mrs. Bennet finished, shaking her handkerchief in a way that signaled an attack of her nerves was sure to follow. "Mr. Collins will not even dine with us this evening, so you cannot hope to win him back. Ungracious, headstrong girl!"

"We can have an evening free from his droning?" Kitty asked, looking hopeful. She and Lydia exchanged gleeful looks.

"Where is he to go instead?" Mary asked.

"He is to dine with the Lucas'. What he expects to find there is beyond me, for Lady Lucas has never set a table as fine as ours, and Sir Lucas is notoriously stingy with the meat. Let this be a lesson to you," Mrs. Bennet cried, shaking her finger at Mary, Kitty, and Lydia. "Men do not take lightly to being offended, and you never know when another offer will come your way," she shot a dark look at Elizabeth, "or if another man will ever offer for you at all!"

"Is it not better to reject a man honestly, knowing the marriage would not be a happy one, than to marry for security only?" Mary asked. "Mr. Collins behaved poorly as well, to force the issue when Papa cannot be consulted for his consent."

"Oh, be quiet, Mary," Mrs. Bennet snapped. Mary shrugged and went back to playing the pianoforte, seemingly unconcerned with the censure.

Elizabeth considered presenting the news that Mr. Bennet had opened his eyes that morning, but decided against it. It would do no good to create false hope. Instead she leaned back and considered Mr. Darcy's proposal. She wouldn't think about her father just now. No, she would imagine just what

Mrs. Bennet would have to say if she ever learned her daughter had refused a man who had ten thousand pounds a year, and in a way that most certainly had offended him.

℘

Not until that evening, when Jane and Elizabeth were closeted in their own room and preparing for bed, did Elizabeth bring up the incident with her father.

"Oh, Lizzy, that is the best news," Jane said immediately. "I am so glad you went to Netherfield this morning, even if my mother was upset with you. The uncertainty is so hard on her, but I am sure she appreciates you tending to father as well."

Elizabeth gave an unladylike snort. "Yes, I am certain that is why she proceeded to tell me that I was selfish, ungrateful, and wild for making the trip this morning. Oh, Jane, don't look like that. I know my mother means well, and I am not upset by her actions. It is no secret that I am not her favorite daughter, and I never have been."

"You are my father's favorite," Jane replied, her beautiful face still wrinkled with lines of concern. "Even if my mother does not understand, I know that is why you went to him again today. For all that I love him and worry about our future if—if we can no longer live at Longbourn, it must be worse for you. I am so glad there is good news."

Elizabeth did not want to think about the worst that could happen, much less talk about it. "Jane, do not assume what happened this morning means my father will recover. The nurse was quite adamant that it could just as easily mean nothing. He is still in God's hands, and we do not know His plan."

"Still, it is good to hear any news," Jane said. She paused. "Did anything else happen this morning, Lizzy? You looked so upset when you came in, but I did not think it wise to ask in front of Mama."

Images of her morning flashed through Elizabeth's mind. Her father's eyes, the nurse's concern, Mr. Darcy's white face. She had always dreamed of the day when she could tell Jane all the details of her proposal, and now there were two she would rather forget.

Still, Elizabeth wavered at the idea of confessing all to her sister. But no, whatever pain and discomfort she felt would be twice as bad for Jane's gentle heart, and to speak of Mr. Darcy would only lead to Mr. Bingley, a subject Elizabeth was especially keen to avoid after knowing of Mr. Darcy's interference. She did not remember ever keeping a secret from Jane before, and Elizabeth could not help but feel cross with Mr. Darcy for being the cause.

Jane frowned at her slightly, and Elizabeth immediately forced a smile for her sister. "Forgive me, I am tired. I was simply concerned of my reception, both from my mother and Mr. Collins. I know you approved of my visit to Netherfield, but as I was expressly told to not go, I did not imagine making a pleasant entrance."

"I enjoyed that supper was only our usual family party tonight," Jane remarked. "It was pleasant to converse as we are more accustomed to doing."

Elizabeth laughed. "You mean that you were relieved that Mr. Collins was away and we did not have to put up with his—" She broke off abruptly, cocking her head to hear better. "Did you hear that?"

"What do you—" Jane stopped as well as the noise came again.

This time Elizabeth was certain. "Someone is at the door," she said, reaching for a dressing gown and donning it hastily. Not waiting for Jane, Elizabeth hurried out of the room and down the stairs, arriving at the front door just as Mr. Hall, the butler, was opening it.

The person on the other side was a servant from Netherfield, holding a note in one hand. Seeing Elizabeth's worried face, he gave a slight smile and handed the note to Mr. Hall. "It's Mr. Bennet," he said, his smile growing as more of the Bennet sisters appeared behind Elizabeth on the stairs. "He's awake."

Chapter Eleven

Mr. Bennet returned home the next morning, delivered to Longbourn's door in Bingley's carriage. He was accompanied by Mrs. Chrisley, who was to stay for another few days, and Mr. Bingley on horseback. Elizabeth had watched intently for Mr. Darcy's horse when the party first appeared, but he had not joined his friend. Waiting for her father to disembark from the carriage, Elizabeth reflected that she could not blame his absence.

The crowd that waited for Mr. Bennet on the steps was a lively one. Mrs. Bennet was overjoyed that their immediate future was once again secure, Kitty and Lydia foresaw the return of outings and officers, and the older three girls were simply glad their father was well once again. Only Mr. Collins darkened the mood, looking quite gloomy and frowning when he thought no one was watching him. Elizabeth, noting his reaction, took amusement from the display and joy from the fact that she could laugh at such behavior with her father again.

Mr. Bingley did not linger once Mr. Bennet had made his way into the house, going directly to his room to rest after the journey home. He bid them farewell, expressed his wishes for Mr. Bennet's expedient recovery, cast a final look at Jane, and was gone. Worried as she was over her father's weakness, Elizabeth noted the hastily masked sorrow on Jane's face, and silently cursed Mr. Darcy's interference once again.

Mr. Collins did not remain for long either, stating that Mr. Bennet should be left to his immediate family party to recover. He managed to insert four different suggestions that Lady Catherine had offered on the best ways to rest before finally leaving. Once he was gone, Mr. Bennet smiled at Elizabeth. "It seems to me that Lady Catherine would be better off restricting her advice and simply letting those she advises rest in peace. I should wear myself out trying to stay indoors by the fire and take refreshing walks outside at the same time."

Mrs. Bennet scowled at her husband. "Oh, Mr. Bennet! Do not encourage Lizzy! Just wait until you hear what she has done now. She will be the ruin of this family, just you wait and see!"

"Mr. Collins proposed to Lizzy at the ball, and she said she couldn't give him an answer while you were asleep, and then he tried to force the issue and she refused to marry him!" Lydia burst out, looking proud that she had been the one to break the news.

Mr. Bennet's eyes widened and he looked at Elizabeth. "Is that the truth, Lizzy?"

She hesitated, thinking about Lady Catherine's visit and Mr. Darcy interfering when Mr. Collins would have struck her. Good lord, had he considered himself in love with her then? It was all such a mess! She colored, remembered herself, and nodded to her father. "It is, Papa."

"You have upset your mother greatly, Lizzy," Mr. Bennet said.

"Forgive me, Papa, but I could not marry him—I couldn't. Even if he would have waited for your consent, we would have made each other miserable."

Mr. Bennet gave the barest hint of a smile, and relief washed over Elizabeth. "I agree. It is not a marriage I would have endorsed or permitted, and I will not," he raised his voice as Mrs. Bennet began to protest, "hear any more about it at the moment. I intend to rest, and I cannot do so with all of you here clucking like chickens."

Mrs. Bennet continued to grumble, but she shooed her daughters out of the room until at last only Mrs. Chrisley and Elizabeth remained. The latter beamed at her father. "Would you like to hear what is in the paper today, Papa?" she asked.

Her father smiled back, looking tired but content. "I would like that very much. Thank you, Lizzy."

The Bennet household settled back into a routine over the next few days. Jane lacked her usual spirits after learning that the Netherfield party had departed for Town with no set date for their return. Lydia and Kitty walked to Meryton daily and talked of nothing but officers. Mary played the piano. Mrs. Bennet flew into a fit of nerves upon hearing that Mr. Collins had proposed to Charlotte Lucas, who had accepted him. She would not talk to Elizabeth, who was spending most of her days with her father and did not consider the snub worth much attention.

Only on her walks each morning, when most of the household was still abed, did Elizabeth consider how different life felt from the days leading up to the Netherfield ball, when everyone had been filled with anticipation, Jane was basked with the glow of new love, and all seemed right with the world. And even then, Elizabeth never let herself admit how much she wished they could return to those days.

The letter arrived a week after the Netherfield party had departed. Mrs. Hill brought it into Mr. Bennet's study, where he and Elizabeth were discussing the day's paper. He felt well enough to spend days in his chair now, joining them for most meals and making his way around the house much as he had before, if somewhat slower now. Mrs.

Chrisley had departed, pleased with her patient's progress, but Elizabeth had continued to read parts of the paper aloud to her father each day as he rested his eyes.

"Here, Miss Elizabeth," Mrs. Hill said, holding out the letter. She delivered several other pieces of mail to Mr. Bennet, then left them alone again.

"Who has written you, Lizzy?" Mr. Bennet asked, his eyes on a letter he had just opened.

"I don't know," Elizabeth replied slowly, causing her father to look up sharply. The address was written in a pretty, elegant hand, clearly the writing of a female, but not a script she recognized. She turned the letter over, but the back offered no more hints than the front had. "If you do not mind, Papa, I will take this out to the garden to read."

He waved her off. "Go. Leave an old man to his correspondence and enjoy yours. We can finish our discussion later."

She gave him a quick smile and left, hurrying out into the garden far enough that her sisters were unlikely to interrupt, then tore the letter open.

Miss Elizabeth,

I hope you will forgive me the impertinence of writing to you when we have not yet been introduced, but I find I cannot stay silent on this matter. There is too much at stake, and from the great deal I have heard of you, I believe you will agree with me once all is explained.

But I get ahead of myself. Let me begin at the beginning. My name is Georgiana Darcy, younger sister and ward of Fitzwilliam Darcy, whose acquaintance you recently made in Hertfordshire. From what else he has said, you may not have the best impression of me, and I can only pray you will give me the chance to explain my side—our side—of the story to you and read these words with an open mind. Beyond that, all I ask is that you show this to no one and burn it when you have finished reading. You will understand, I believe, once you have read all.

I have two messages to convey in this letter. One pertains more towards my brother; the other, myself. I will start with my story, in the hope that it will put his into context. I am sixteen years old, as you may or may not be aware, and for most of my life have lived a sheltered existence. I have not yet come out in society, and do not wish to do so for several years, since I am shy and uncomfortable around those I do not know. I tell you this so you understand the foundations of the story I am about to relate.

One of those whom I always felt comfortable around was a man of my brother's age by the name of George Wickham. I have gathered from my brother that you have made Mr. Wickham's acquaintance; what you know or think of him beyond that fact I will not attempt to guess. Growing up, I saw Mr. Wickham as a second older brother, one more likely than Fitzwilliam to bend the rules and indulge me in whatever treat I could imagine. We grew apart when he and my brother left for school and I started to become a young lady, but I always thought of him with pleasure and fond memories.

Mr. Wickham came back into my life last summer, when I was staying in Ramsgate with my companion—my previous companion, I should say. This is hard for me to write, even now, so I will tell you the facts as succinctly as I can. Mr. Wickham and my

*companion conspired to bring him
into my company daily. He flattered
me, spoke of love to me, and ultimately
convinced me to elope with him. Had
Fitzwilliam not arrived unexpectedly
to visit, I would have done so. When
the situation was finally laid bare, it
became obvious that Mr. Wickham
cared little for me and much for my
dowry, which is thirty thousand
pounds. I believe he also saw me as a
way to get revenge on my brother,
who has always inspired a good
degree of jealousy in Mr. Wickham.*

*I will reiterate that you do not know
me, and I cannot know your
relationship with Mr. Wickham or
what he may have told you. I can only
trust what I have heard about you,
which is likely far more than you
believe and has lead me to think that
you will be fair and rational in your
judgment of my words. This brings me
to the second purpose of my letter,
which, while bringing me far less
distress, is ultimately harder to write
for it is not of my own pain or
foolishness of which I must speak. I
also have less hard facts to include.*

My brother returned to Town in the worst mood I have seen him in since the days immediately following his arrival at Ramsgate, and that rivaled even the occasions on which our parents died. He did his best to hide his lack of spirits from me, and it was only with a great deal of questions and conversation seemingly on other subjects that I began to understand the truth of his emotions. Of this fact I am sure: my brother believes he behaved so atrociously while in Hertfordshire that he has lost his one true chance at happiness—you. What he did, or believes he did, I do not know. I am biased to believe my brother is the best of men and cannot connect the word "atrocious" to him even when I try, but it is certainly what he thinks.

You may think me impertinent and forward for penning such a letter, but I could not sit by and watch my brother's distress passively when I owe him all the happiness in my life. After my experiences, neither will I attempt to understand all that goes on between a man and woman, and if he did you a grave injustice or you are truly opposed to him, let me know and

*I shall say no more ever again. You
need not even reply—should I not hear
from you, I will know what to think,
and I apologize for any distress I have
caused you. But if you are uncertain,
or have been told falsehoods by a man
with a sweet voice and a jealous heart,
then know this: my brother loves you,
Miss Elizabeth. I have never seen him
so affected before, and I will not guess
if I shall ever again.*

Most respectfully yours,

Georgiana Darcy

Elizabeth stared at the letter, unsure of the emotions swirling through her, for long minutes. She read it once more, then again. Finally, deciding that a walk may help her sort through her thoughts with greater success, she stood and looked up, her eyes falling on perhaps the most unwelcome face that could have appeared in that moment, only yards away and coming quickly towards her.

"Mr. Wickham!"

Chapter Twelve

"Miss Elizabeth, you look as lovely as ever," Mr. Wickham pronounced as he came up to her.

On a normal day, she would have had a witty return for him, but today was anything but normal. "Mr. Wickham," she replied simply instead, folding the letter as inconspicuously as she could and tucking it rather further into her sleeve than she would have done with a normal missive.

"You are still lacking in the spirits that make you so irresistible," he observed, bowing over her hand. "Do not fear, my dearest, your fortunes must soon improve. Shall I accompany you home?" he gestured towards Longbourn with his free hand.

Elizabeth withdrew her hand sharply. "I am not your anything, Mr. Wickham, and I will not allow privileges. If you will not respect that, then I believe we must part ways at once."

"You could be my everything, dear Elizabeth," he persisted. "For you, I would conquer the world."

"Mr. Wickham, you do not have the right to call me by my Christian name." Thinking to nip the conversation in the bud without being outright rude, she continued, "I apologize, but I am not in the mood for conversation today. I am sure you will understand that I do not mean offense when I ask you to leave me to myself. As you so astutely noted, I am still not returned to my usual spirits."

"Then we must indeed say goodbye, for I leave town tomorrow. I had hoped to take you with me and start a better life for both of us. Say you'll come, my lovely Elizabeth. We could be in Gretna Green by Wednesday."

Elizabeth was far from persuaded. Instead, the thought crossed her mind that Mr. Wickham must offer marriage to anything in skirts, for she had little to offer in the way of money, and though their conversations had often been laced with small flirtations, she had thought it understood that friendship was all they would find in each other. In light of the letter from Georgiana—whose word she did not question despite not knowing the lady—Mr. Wickham's insensible advances were rendered even more undesirable.

"Mr. Wickham, you have misjudged my character gravely if you think I would welcome such advances.

You insult me with the suggestion that I begin a marriage without my family's approval, indeed by running away with no warning! I have made my feelings very clear on marrying without my father's permission, and *that* union was with my cousin and my father's heir, not a relatively new acquaintance with only his own word to recommend himself. As knowledgeable as you seem about the events of the Netherfield ball and its aftermath, I cannot imagine you were ignorant of my sentiments. Therefore, I can only conclude you have taken leave of your senses, and I intend to end this conversation before you say anything else that we both may regret. Farewell, sir."

She walked purposely towards Longbourn, not looking back to see how he reacted. The cad did not deserve her sympathies, she thought bitterly, folding her arms so she could feel the letter tucked into her sleeve. It would not do to lose it where the man it condemned might happen across it—or where one of her foolish sisters could do the same and spread the gossip it contained.

Beyond her annoyance, she was surprisingly unaffected by the conversation. In fact, Elizabeth decided as she made her way in the back door and swiftly up the stairs, Mr. Wickham's proposal was the least distressing by far. It took her very little effort to put the event from her mind, especially once she had closed her bedroom door, gone directly to the window where the light was best, and sat down to read her letter again.

Elizabeth waited until the letter had turned fully to ash before she left her room in search of Jane. She had read it until her eyes blurred, committing every word to memory and pondering what Georgiana must have thought while writing it. *My brother loves you, Miss Elizabeth. I have never seen him so affected before. My brother loves you. If you have been told falsehoods by a man with a sweet voice and a jealous heart, know this.*

It had occurred to Elizabeth, in the long minutes that she poured over every word and nuance in the letter, to doubt Georgiana or question whether Mr. Darcy had put his sister up to the task. She had dismissed the latter idea almost as soon as it appeared in her mind, though—Mr. Darcy, arrogant man that he was, had never once showed a lack of honor. As for the former, she had similarly failed to come up with a reason why any young woman would tell such a horrid lie about herself, one that would most certainly ruin her if it was generally known. She was also ashamed to recognize qualities in Mr. Wickham which matched those that Georgiana detailed, qualities Elizabeth herself had ignored or listed as social niceties in the time that she had known the man, seeing him as far preferable to the terse Mr. Darcy.

If you have been told falsehoods by a man with a sweet voice and a jealous heart, know this.

The shame had grown slowly as the contents of the letter took time to truly sink in, but once Elizabeth understood just how wrong her assumptions had been, she could feel little else. Mr. Darcy had proposed—horribly, yes, but he had opened his heart to her nonetheless—and she had not only thrown Mr. Wickham in his face as a reason for rejecting him, but told him she would rather accept the man he had every reason to hate. Oh, no wonder he was so affected, and how naive he must find her now!

Well, it was too late to regret how she acted. She would likely never see Mr. Darcy again, and had no expectation of civility even if she did. All that remained to her was to learn from her mistakes and curb her tongue in the future. But she could not keep the entire story to herself; once again, it was too much to bear. She would not betray Georgiana's confidences, or go against the girl's request to show the letter to no one. However, Elizabeth owed Jane an account of Mr. Darcy's proposal now that the anger of the moment had faded, and in order to make the story complete there was information from the letter she would have to include.

Leaving her own room, Elizabeth paused as she considered where her sister was most likely to be found. In a stroke of luck, for she did not wish to appear in the sitting room in her current state of mind, Jane appeared at the top of the stairs.

"Lizzy, there you are. I was just coming to find you—are you feeling well? Is it another headache?"

Of course she had a headache; Elizabeth thought she'd had one since the moment Mr. Darcy asked her to dance at Netherfield. But saying that to Jane would only make her worry, so she shook her head. "I am well. I was coming to find you, though. Perhaps we can talk here?"

Jane quickly acquiesced and followed Elizabeth into their room. "Is there something in particular that you would like to talk about?"

Settling herself on the end of Jane's bed, Elizabeth gave her sister a rueful smile. "Oh, yes. Make yourself comfortable, sister mine. I have a story to tell you, and I fear it will take some time."

&

By the time Elizabeth was done with her story and she and Jane had discussed all of it in turn, the afternoon had turned to evening and it was nearly time for supper. Since they were at home with no visitors, the ladies did not bother changing for the evening meal. Instead, they made their way to the sitting room, where their mother and younger sisters were gathered.

"Oh, there you are!" Mrs. Bennet exclaimed, exasperated. "I declare, Lizzy, your rogue habits will be the death of me. Have you no care for my nerves!"

Elizabeth exchanged a quick look with Jane, who gave a sympathetic smile in response. "What have I done to distress you now, Mama?" she asked, crossing to sit at a chair just outside the main circle.

"You were gone yet again, running off with no care for any of the rest of us, and unable to receive callers! Mr. Wickham asked for you by name, and was most disappointed when you did not appear!"

Elizabeth's mind spun as thoughts flew through it. So that was why Betsey had come to see where she was—she had sent the maid away using the excuse of a headache without a second thought. And the nerve of Mr. Wickham, to inquire after her when she had been more than plain in her desire to avoid conversation with him!

She opened her mouth to repeat her headache excuse, but Mrs. Bennet continued on. "I know you care not for the good of your family, but surely you must understand that you will need a husband. How are you to find one if you avoid or offend all the gentlemen callers we receive?"

Any sympathy Elizabeth felt for her mother's situation disappeared. "And how would someone like Mr. Wickham support me, if we were to wed?" she asked sharply. "He has made it quite clear that he has little money and no expectation of gaining

115

more." Thinking that this may be an effective way to warn her sisters about the man without betraying Georgiana or raising suspicion of where she had gained her insights, she went on, "Besides, we have only known the man for a matter of weeks. Who can say what he is truly like, or if he would indeed make a good husband? I have seen him flatter far too many ladies to believe him capable of true loyalty for long."

"Oh, la, Lizzy, you jest!" Lydia broke in, tossing her hair. "You are too serious. Mr. Wickham is the best of men, anyone can see that. He has been horribly treated and wants only to avoid causing others the same pain." Her eyes narrowed. "I thought you liked him, better than any other man of your acquaintance."

"I did like him," Elizabeth responded. "That does not mean I think him a wise person to marry, and I do not like him so much that I am blind to the possibility of unknown faults."

"Oh, you *did* like him?" Lydia pressed, stressing the past tense. "Are you done with him, then? I'll gladly take him from you—he's the most handsome of all the officers in town!" She grinned at Kitty and the pair burst out in giggles. Mrs. Bennet joined in while Mary looked quite put out and Jane and Elizabeth exchanged another worried glance.

"Aren't you a bit young to be thinking of marriage, Lydia?" Jane asked in her sweet voice. "You would not want to choose one man now when there are so many more you are sure to meet, men worth waiting for." From the look on her face, Elizabeth knew her sister was thinking of Mr. Bingley.

Lydia only laughed more. "I'm fifteen, that's old enough!" she exclaimed. "Why, I would be ashamed to turn twenty without a husband. Just you wait, I'll be the first to marry out of all of us."

On that note, Mrs. Hill came to announce that supper was ready, and try though she might, Elizabeth could not think of a way to get through to her headstrong, foolish sister. It seemed that she would have more than one reason to be grateful for Mr. Wickham's decision to leave town.

&

Most of the family was at breakfast the next morning when Kitty flew into the room, looking quite put out. "Have you seen Lydia? She hasn't gone to visit Mrs. Forster without me, surely? She talked about going last night, but she promised to wait for me!"

"Calm yourself, Kitty, she is likely still in bed," Mr. Bennet replied, not looking up from his paper. "You girls can go to Meryton after breakfast."

"But she's not, she isn't in bed!" Kitty exclaimed. "I checked, pulled back her covers and everything. She isn't there, and her new hat is missing."

Now Mr. Bennet looked up, folding the paper and laying it aside. He looked around at the rest of the family, eyes narrowing. "Have any of you girls seen your sister this morning?"

"No, Papa."

"No."

"Not since last night, Papa."

"Mrs. Bennet?" he asked, looking to his wife. "Have you heard of any schemes that might have led Lydia from the house?"

When Mrs. Bennet shook her head, he turned back to Kitty and fixed her with a sharp look. "And you, Catherine, have you heard of any other plans from your sister?"

Kitty's bottom lip slid out in an indignant pout. "No, she hasn't told me anything since she started spending time with Mrs. Forster. You should ask *her*, if you don't find Lydia with her when you get there!" Turning on her heel, she left the room at a run.

A servant was soon dispatched to town, but Lydia was not to be found at Mrs. Forster's house. Neither was she with her Aunt Phillips, or in any of the

Meryton shops. A search of her room revealed more missing items than just her newest hat, and in only a few hours the search for the youngest Bennet was frantic indeed.

"But where?" Mrs. Bennet kept repeating. "Where is Lydia, and why would she leave us like this?"

Elizabeth closed her eyes and prayed she didn't know.

Chapter Thirteen

Dear Miss Darcy,

This is not the letter I had hoped to write you, although I can hardly imagine what I would have said, had circumstances indeed been different, and I cannot imagine this letter will be any easier for you to read than it is for me to write. Be glad you have not yet made my acquaintance, for you shall not have to suffer through my misfortunes and are protected from my circumstances impacting you in any way. I will follow your standard and state the facts plainly, as I know them. I apologize if I do not make sense, for I find I can scarcely complete a coherent thought.

My youngest sister, Lydia, has been missing for the past two and a half days. We have only a note to guide us, left for her friend to find once she was gone. She has disappeared, eloped, thrown herself upon the mercies of none other than George Wickham— and not a day after he had made me a similar offer. It was uninvited, I assure you, and would have been rejected even before I heard your story. I owe your brother quite an apology, for Mr. Wickham deceived me fully, and it was only in the last week that I began to see through his façade. When your letter arrived and I had confirmation of my new suspicions, I tried to impart some of the same wisdom to my sisters without betraying your confidences, but Lydia is not the type of girl to heed warnings. She is but fifteen and I regret to say that our parents have not checked her as they might have done, which has led her to be headstrong and foolish, thinking only of her present joys. Do not assume she was an unwilling participant in this situation.

Unwise as a marriage would be between Mr. Wickham and my sister, we are currently most desperate to

*ensure it has taken place, though I
have little faith that it has or ever will.
His acquaintances in the militia report
with no hesitation that Mr. Wickham
would not have married a girl with so
little to offer. My father has gone to
London, where he will enlist the help
of my uncle, but I expect little success
from either. She is lost to us forever,
and we are ruined. So you see, Miss
Darcy, you should rejoice in our lack
of connection.*

*Those sentiments aside, I thank you
for your letter. I have burned it as you
asked, and am certain that no one laid
eyes upon it other than myself. From
the time that I broke the seal until I
saw it turn to ash, it did not leave my
person. You needn't fear that you
offended me; I thank you for your care
and only regret that this must be my
reply.*

*I will ask in return that you do not
spread word of Lydia's situation until
it is certain that she is lost. I do not
doubt such an outcome and know that
the truth cannot be concealed for long,
but will you think me foolish if I relish
in knowing that I have a handful of
days remaining to me where I am not*

*universally scorned by society? It
does little good, for we have not left
the house since Lydia's deceit was
discovered, but it brings me some
comfort nonetheless. If by some
miraculous chance Lydia is recovered
or her marriage can be confirmed, I
will send word so you know how this
story ends. If that day never comes,
then I shall remember your words
kindly. I imagine I will spend a good
many of the coming days reflecting on
what might have been, and you shall
add sweetness to such fantasies.*

Sincerely,

Elizabeth Bennet

Elizabeth sighed and put down her pen, waiting longer than necessary for the ink to dry before she folded and addressed the letter. She would not tell anyone of her letter to Georgiana—not even Jane, who knew of the original letter. There was nothing to be gained from sharing the correspondence, and Mrs. Bennet would be impossible to silence if she found out that her daughter was writing to a Darcy, never mind the fact that the letter was likely to be the last the pair ever exchanged. No, her mother would see it as a sign that the family was saved, as if marriage to a wealthy man could wash away the blemish Lydia had put on all of their names.

The sigh turned to a frown. Mrs. Bennet was being stubbornly obtuse even for her, refusing to recognize that Lydia was likely gone for good and in her wake the remaining four daughters had lost whatever social standing they held previously. Elizabeth had walked out of her mother's room yesterday at Mrs. Bennet's insistence that wedding clothes be purchased for her youngest daughter and a wedding breakfast planned for the newlyweds when they reappeared in Hertfordshire. She had yet to return.

Kitty was nearly as inconsolable. She seemed to have a better grasp on the reality of the situation than her mother, but that Lydia should have left her to the drudgery of Longbourn without so much as a hint of her plans had hit her hard. The note they unearthed was addressed to Mrs. Forster, not herself, and had even called the former "my dearest friend." To say that Kitty felt quite sorry for herself was no understatement.

Elizabeth did not find her second-youngest sister's distress to be necessarily bad. Should Lydia be recovered, then Kitty may well fare better in society without her poor influence. If Lydia was indeed not recovered, which seemed more likely every day, then society's opinion would be forever tainted anyway—but Elizabeth recognized that Lydia's disappearance and Kitty's disillusionment with her younger sister's actions could be the key to Kitty becoming a more refined, well-behaved young lady.

If only Lydia were to be found! Mr. Bennet had left for London almost immediately after Mrs. Forster discovered the note, but so far his reports contained no good news. Elizabeth frowned again. The reports—of which there had been two—were only a few lines each, containing barely enough information to warrant sending. Combined, they said only that Mr. Bennet had reached London. He had found no word of the pair at Epsom or Clapham, but continued to believe they had gone to London, not Gretna Green. Beyond that, he had little idea of where to start but would attempt to search for Lydia and Mr. Wickham over the next few days nonetheless. To make matters worse, each day brought more information on the debts Wickham had left behind him in Meryton. It was hopeless.

But thinking would do no good, so Elizabeth stood and picked up her letter. It needed to be sent—and then, personal feelings aside, she would go to her mother so Jane could rest.

&

Mr. Bennet returned home a week later with no more news. Even Jane, perpetually positive, rose each morning with less and less hope in the days following his return. Elizabeth, in the midst of her could-have-been daydreams, had begun to think more practically of employment. She had read well, but enough to be a governess? She spoke French—poorly—but had no knowledge of Latin, Italian, Spanish, or German. Geography would be easy to explain; she loved maps. History could be turned into an intriguing narrative. Her musical talents were mediocre at best, and while she could sew a tight seam or turn a hem with ease, she had never put in enough practice to be truly good at the decorative stitches favored by ladies who could employ a governess for their education.

A ladies' companion required less skills, but they were typically widowed women who could be expected to chaperone their charges effectively. *Well*, Elizabeth thought, making a face at her reflection in the window pane, *that is the idea*. Her thoughts turned to Miss Darcy's former companion, who had clearly put her own ambitions ahead of Georgiana's well-being and reputation. Elizabeth frowned. She couldn't imagine Mr. Darcy putting just anyone in charge of his sister. Had Mrs. Younge come with recommendations? Would her own lack of experience effectively cut off this career option as well?

Without realizing what she did, her hands came up to massage her temples. The constant headache she had experienced since Lydia's elopement threatened to send her back to her room for an afternoon of rest, and after two weeks of remaining indoors, the idea of resting more was nearly enough to drive her mad. How she longed for one of her long walks! Leaning back in her chair, Elizabeth forced herself to relax in the hopes that the headache would recede with the tension all down her spine.

Opening her eyes, she gasped and jumped up, all thoughts of resting forgotten. Ignoring her now pounding headache, she ran for the door.

"Lizzy!" Mary exclaimed from the pianoforte.

"An express, there's an express rider coming down the lane," Elizabeth cried, not pausing. As she quit the room, she could hear noises indicating that Mary and Kitty—Jane was once again with her mother in Mrs. Bennet's bedroom—were following her. "Papa," Elizabeth cried as she passed his book room, but did not stop there either. Only when she had exited the front door did she pause, heart beating wildly in her chest.

The rider pulled his horse to a stop several paces away. "I have a letter for Mr. Thomas Bennet of Longbourn," he said formally.

"That is me," Mr. Bennet said from behind Elizabeth. She, Mary, and Kitty all moved aside so he could pass between them and take the letter. "Is a response required?"

"It is," the rider replied, and Elizabeth's heart gave a wild thump. She craned her neck to get a look at the handwriting on the letter, but her father's hand effectively obscured it. What news would require both an express and a response? Oh, she couldn't hope that the letter contained good news. It would hurt too much when the truth was revealed.

"Very well," Mr. Bennet said. "If you take your horse to the stables, he will be seen to and the cook will find something for you while you wait."

The man inclined his head and rode off in the direction of the stable.

"Who is it from, Papa?"

"What does it say?"

"Is it about Lydia?"

Elizabeth, Kitty, and Mary spoke over each other, all staring at their father intently. Frowning at them, he broke open the seal on the letter and scanned it, revealing the handwriting on the address.

"It is from Uncle!" Elizabeth exclaimed. "Has he found her?"

Jane appeared on the steps. "What has happened? Is there news?"

Mr. Bennet's frown deepened. "He has found them. They were in London, as we suspected."

"Both of them! Then they are married!"

"Yes, both of them. They are *not* married, Jane. I can hardly believe what he says. Here, Lizzy, read it aloud for us so all questions are satisfied at once."

Elizabeth grasped the letter and began to read aloud rapidly.

> *My Dear Brother,*
>
> *At last I am able to send you some tidings of my niece, and such as, upon the whole, I hope will give you satisfaction. Soon after you left me on Saturday, I was fortunate enough to find out in what part of London they were. The particulars I reserve till we meet. It is enough to know they are discovered. I have seen them both. They are not married, nor can I find there was any intention of being so; but if you are willing to perform the engagements which I have ventured to make on your side, I hope it will not be long before they are.*
>
> *All that is required of you is to assure to your daughter, by settlement, her equal share of the five thousand pounds secured among your children after the decease of yourself and my sister; and, moreover, to enter into an*

engagement of allowing her, during your life, one hundred pounds per annum. These are conditions which, considering everything, I had no hesitation in complying with, as far as I thought myself privileged, for you. I shall send this by express, that no time may be lost in bringing me your answer.

You will easily comprehend, from these particulars, that Mr. Wickham's circumstances are not so hopeless as they are generally believed to be. The world has been deceived in that respect; and, I am happy to say, there will be some little money, even when all his debts are discharged, to settle on my niece, in addition to her own fortune. If, as I conclude will be the case, you send me full powers to act in your name throughout the whole of this business, I will immediately give directions to Haggerston for preparing a proper settlement.

There will not be the smallest occasion for your coming to town again; therefore, stay quietly at Longbourn, and depend on my diligence and care. Send back your answer as soon as you can, and be

*careful to write explicitly. We have
judged it best that my niece should be
married from this house, of which I
hope you will approve. She comes to
us to-day. I shall write again as soon
as anything more is determined on.*

Edward Gardiner

For a moment after Elizabeth finished reading, there was silence in the entryway. Then voices erupted.

"They are to be married!"

"We are saved!"

"But how?"

"I must tell Mama!"

"You will agree, Papa, surely?"

Mr. Bennet reclaimed the letter and walked away in the direction of his book room without saying a thing. Elizabeth followed him. Only when the door closed behind them did she repeat her question.

"Oh yes, there is little for me to do but agree," he said. "I hate to do so, though, knowing what your uncle must have done for Lydia."

"What do you mean?" she exclaimed.

Mr. Bennet held the letter up and gave it a slight shake. "I feel that there is much he doesn't say. Enough money to settle his debts and for them to live on? And to accept a girl with only a thousand pounds? I may be little inclined to attend to my daughters as I ought, but I am not a fool through and through. This is not the entirety of the deal your uncle has made, and I cannot pay him back. Never forget this, Lizzy. Whatever he did, your uncle has saved this family."

Chapter Fourteen

Mrs. Lydia Wickham arrived at her old home on the first day of the new year with the air of a queen bestowing a great honor upon her subjects. She sailed from the carriage, barely sparing a sideways glance for Kitty, who had rushed out to meet her, and instead went straight to her mother.

"Oh look, Mama, is my ring not gorgeous?" she asked, extending her hand as if expecting Mrs. Bennet to kiss it. Turning to smile at Mr. Wickham, she added, "And I am so fortunate to have a handsome husband to go with it. I declare, I shall pray daily that my sisters are as lucky as I have been!"

Elizabeth, standing at the rear of the group, was caught between rolling her eyes and storming away in anger. Lydia was as lax with her prayers as she was with any subject not revolving around a handsome face or a red coat, and to insinuate that her sisters should want to imitate her situation was so horridly wrong Elizabeth nearly found the statement laughable.

But Mrs. Bennet was exclaiming over the ring, all of her thoughts focused on the glitter and sparkle and excitement of having her favorite daughter returned and married.

"You are lucky indeed!" she exclaimed. "To be married at fifteen, and to an officer too! Oh, you must come inside and tell me all about it. We have missed you so much here!"

Struggling to keep her face impassive, Elizabeth thought suddenly of Mr. Darcy and his propensity to show little emotion. What feelings and struggles passed through his mind unknown by those around him? How he must have loathed to hear of Mr. Wickham, knowing that the man had actively tried to ruin his most beloved sister, and yet only on rare occasions had that anger been visible. She had done him a grave disservice by assuming his only emotions were pride and disdain.

Caught up in her thoughts, Elizabeth was left at the back of the party as they turned to go inside. Much to her annoyance, she found Mr. Wickham at her side.

"It is good to see you again, sister," he said, wearing the same gallant expression she had seen so many times before. "Although still not back in your usual spirits, I believe?"

Her parents had deigned to allow the couple back to Longbourn, but *she* did not have to welcome them gladly. "You are correct. It is a fault I lay squarely on your shoulders, *sir,* although I am quite unhappy with my sister as well."

"Don't tell me you are jealous, Elizabeth," he said with a slight leer. "I asked you first, after all."

Elizabeth bristled at his use of her Christian name, though it was now technically proper given his marriage to Lydia. "I never desired a man who moves from woman to woman as it suits his financial and physical needs," she hissed. *And I hope my sister keeps you happy in one regard, Mr. Wickham, for you can be sure she lacks the other—especially compared to Miss Darcy! Do not expect me to be sorry for you when you grow tired of her antics or run out of money.*

Luckily, they had reached the front door, and she slipped in ahead of him, going directly to the sitting room and taking a chair that would not allow him to sit near her. Still, he looked as if he would continue to engage her in conversation when Mrs. Bennet began to exclaim over him, insisting that he take a seat near her. Elizabeth was free to take up her much-neglected sewing and pretend it held her attention until Lydia shoved her ring under Elizabeth's nose.

"La, Lizzy, you look so stern!" she exclaimed, flouncing down on a nearby stool. "You must admire my ring; everyone else has and they find it delightful."

"It is a beautiful ring," Elizabeth said evenly. "I am glad that you are happy to wear it."

Lydia laughed, the sound meant to attract attention. "Oh yes, I am quite ecstatic to wear it. I would have married my dear Wickham without such a ring, but of course it is better with one. I cannot wait to show Maria Lucas—she will be so jealous! But then I always was cleverer than she."

"I hardly call your actions clever," Elizabeth said. "You nearly ruined all of us, do you not understand that?"

"Oh, do hush," Lydia said, petulant. She lowered her voice. "You're nearly as bad as Mr. Darcy. I thought he would ruin my wedding with his long face and dreadfully boring speeches about duty and family."

Elizabeth felt as if someone had dumped a bucket of freezing water over her head. "Mr. Darcy was at your wedding?" she asked, voice even quieter than Lydia's had been.

Her sister looked at her sideways. "I'm not supposed to say," she said primly, turning up her nose in a way meant to be pretty. "I shouldn't have said anything, so I suppose you'll just have to wonder." She jumped up and danced across the room to sit next to Kitty, leaving Elizabeth dumbstruck.

"Lizzy, dearest, are you feeling well?" Jane asked. "You've gone white. Is it another headache?"

Grateful for the excuse, Elizabeth gave a wan smile and stood. "I'm afraid it is. Please do excuse me, I believe I must lay down if I am to join you for supper."

Mrs. Bennet waved her off, uncaring if her least favorite daughter left while Lydia was present to fawn over. Keeping her eyes firmly away from Mr. Wickham, Elizabeth left the room.

Mr. Darcy was at my sister's wedding. Mr. Darcy was at my sister's wedding—to Mr. Wickham, the man he has every reason to hate and avoid. How in the world did he become involved in the situation? And more to the point—why?

&

One benefit of Lydia's marriage was that Elizabeth could once again take her customary long walks. The morning after the Wickhams' arrival, she set out early despite the chilly air and winds. Meandering in the general direction of Oakham Mount, Elizabeth realized that for the first time since her father had collapsed, she had no hint of a headache. She could relax. Her family's home was secure for the time being, all sisters were accounted for, and she could not think of a man who might be waiting around the bend with an ill-advised proposal.

She was not perfectly happy; there was still too much lingering tension for that. Lydia's presence brought about annoyance rather than peace, which was a sentiment that Elizabeth rarely felt around members of her family other than Jane. And of course, Jane herself did not seem either happy or at peace lately, which was far more unusual for her than for Elizabeth. Still, Elizabeth mused as she walked on, her plaguing headaches had truly disappeared in the night. Surely that boded for better times ahead.

Elizabeth reached Oakham Mount in good time despite her slower-than-usual pace. She lingered on the peak, enjoying the view and the feeling of being outside in solitude once again. Finally, the wind became too cold to bear, and she turned back towards home and the shelter of the trees below the mount.

Walking back towards Longbourn brought up all of her unanswered questions as she considered once again the inhabitants and how they had come to be there in their current state. It also reminded her of a promise she needed to fulfil.

I'll write to Georgiana and tell her how Lydia's story ends—or at least where it stands currently—but I won't ask about her brother in case Lydia was wrong or Georgiana doesn't know of his involvement, she decided. *And then I'll write to my aunt and see if she knows how Mr. Darcy plays into Lydia's miraculous recovery. Something is missing from the story, and it wouldn't surprise me at all if Mr. Darcy is the key.*

&

My Dear Niece,

I have just received your letter, and shall devote this whole morning to answering it, as I foresee that a little writing will not comprise what I have to tell you. I must confess myself surprised by your application; I did not expect it from you. Don't think me angry, however, for I only mean to let you know that I had not imagined such enquiries to be necessary on your side. If you do not choose to understand me, forgive my impertinence. Your uncle is as much surprised as I am—he expected something quite different based on his recent conversations. But if you are really innocent and ignorant, I must be more explicit.

On the very day of your father's return to Longbourn, your uncle had a most unexpected visitor. Mr. Darcy called, as you may have guessed, and

*was shut up with him several hours.
He came to tell Mr. Gardiner that he
had found out where your sister and
Mr. Wickham were, and that he had
seen and talked with them both;
Wickham repeatedly, Lydia once. The
motive professed for his involvement
in the search was his conviction of its
owing to himself that Wickham's
worthlessness had not been so well
known as to make it impossible for any
young woman of character to love or
confide in him. He generously
imputed the whole to his mistaken
pride, and confessed that he had
before thought it beneath him to lay
his private actions open to the world.
His character was to speak for itself.
He called it, therefore, his duty to step
forward, and endeavor to remedy an
evil which had been brought on by
himself.*

*This is where my assumption of your
greater knowledge arose, for Mr.
Darcy also made it known that he
became aware of the situation in a
letter you wrote to his sister. While he
asked that Lydia's family not be made
aware of his involvement, he also
commented that you would find the*

*state of affairs intriguing, having
recently taken him to task for many of
the character deficiencies he sought to
remedy and had been, I quote,
"correct as she most always is." Will
you find me more impertinent still if I
confess that I like him very much? But
that is enough of my teasing, there is
more of Lydia's story to tell.*

*Mr. Darcy looked for some days
before he was able to discover them;
but he had something to direct his
search, which was more than we had.
There is a lady, it seems, a Mrs.
Younge, who was some time ago
governess to Miss Darcy, and was
dismissed from her charge on some
cause of disapprobation, though he
did not say what. She then took a
large house in Edward-street, and has
since maintained herself by letting
lodgings. This Mrs. Younge was, he
knew, intimately acquainted with
Wickham; and he went to her for
intelligence of him as soon as he got
to town. It was two or three days
before he could get from her what he
wanted, but in the end she did know
where her friend was to be found.
Wickham indeed had gone to her on*

their first arrival in London, and had
she been able to receive them into her
house, they would have taken up their
abode with her. Though that was not
the case, she knew where they were to
be found.

Mr. Darcy saw both Wickham and
Lydia, and attempted in vain to
convince her to quit her present
situation and return home. But he
found Lydia absolutely resolved on
remaining where she was. She wanted
no help of his; she would not hear of
leaving Wickham. They would be
married eventually, she assumed,
although Mr. Darcy's first
conversation with Wickham proved
this was not his design. When
pressed, he even admitted that he still
hoped to marry a young lady with a
fortune on which they could live.
Circumstances being what they were,
however, Mr. Wickham was willing to
negotiate. Once matters were settled
between the two of them, he came to
call in Gracechurch Street. From
what he knew of your father, he
judged that it might be better to speak
to your uncle alone, and so waited

until your father departed for Longbourn.

He called again on Saturday and was closeted up with your uncle for most of the day. Mr. Darcy was most insistent that he pay the entire amount, though between you and me your uncle would have been happy to settle the whole. They battled it together for a long time, which was more than either the gentleman or lady concerned deserved. In the end your uncle was forced to relent. If Mr. Darcy has a fault, as you have indicated in our past correspondence, it is his stubbornness. I believe your letter this morning gave your uncle great pleasure, because it required an explanation that would rob him of his borrowed feathers, and give the praise where it was due. But, Lizzy, this must go no farther than yourself, or Jane at most. You know pretty well, I suppose, what has been done for the young people. His debts are to be paid, amounting, I believe, to considerably more than a thousand pounds, another thousand in addition to her own settled upon her, and his commission purchased.

There was, of course, a delay in the proceedings due to Christmas. Mr. Darcy delivered Lydia to us before Christmas, and following the holidays he finalized the money matters and was present at the wedding. Your uncle's pride aside, we both enjoyed our interactions with the man. I am much less impressed with the behavior exhibited by the newly married couple. Mr. Wickham acted with no remorse, either seen or relayed by Mr. Darcy. As for Lydia, I talked to her repeatedly in the most serious manner, representing to her all the wickedness of what she had done, and all the unhappiness she had brought on her family. If she heard me, it was by dumb luck, for I am sure she did not listen.

I have now told you the whole of the story, as I understand it. I will end by saying that I look forward to seeing you soon. It is very fortunate that your uncle was able to arrange matters so he can be away from his business and we are able to make our usual Christmas visit, if a bit later than usual. Any questions you have, I will be happy to discuss with you then.

For now, I must write no more. The children have been wanting me this half hour.

Yours, very sincerely,

Madeline Gardiner

Chapter Fifteen

The sentiments relayed in her aunt's letter produced in Elizabeth a strange mix of both satisfaction and distress. At last, she understood the missing piece in Lydia's story, the days that had filled the gap between elopement and actual marriage. On the other hand, her aunt's causally hinted words of Mr. Darcy in regard to herself brought far more pain than Georgiana's direct, open letter ever had. She knew now what type of man he was; to hear her aunt tease and know such a union could never come about left her increasingly regretful and remiss.

Oh, what a life she might have lived with Mr. Darcy, had her pride not blinded her to his finer qualities! He was a gentleman, she recognized now, who would suit her in every way. She could respect his opinion and desires, and in turn bring playfulness and joy to his structured life. But it was not to be. He must surely detest her now, for her words and her unavoidable association with Mr. Wickham. No, whatever Mrs. Gardiner thought she detected could not be true, no matter how much Elizabeth wished otherwise. She did wonder exactly what Mr. Darcy had said—Mrs. Gardiner must truly have mistaken a statement if she was so convinced as to hint at the situation in her letter.

"Enough," Elizabeth murmured to herself under her breath. No good would come from wishing things were different, and whatever she had said to Georgiana, daydreaming about impossible "might have beens" left a sour taste in her mouth. She ought to take a page from Jane's book and try to find the positives in the situation. Her Aunt and Uncle Gardiner would be there soon, and an invitation for a public assembly had been delivered earlier in the day. Mr. Darcy had done her family an incredible amount of good, finding Lydia and seeing her married, and— Elizabeth smiled wryly to herself—she only had to endure Lydia and her new husband for another three days before they removed to the north of England for the foreseeable future. Surely that, if nothing else, was something she could appreciate!

§

The Gardiners came and went, bringing with them their usual cheer. More serious topics of conversation were discussed at the supper table among the adults, and the Bennet girls all did their best to spoil their younger cousins. Mrs. Gardiner spent long afternoons talking to Jane and Elizabeth, although Elizabeth noted that her aunt seemed to spend more effort on involving Mary and Kitty than she had in the past. The week flew by with a great amount of joy and very few mentions of Lydia—or of a dark, handsome man from Derbyshire. Then the Gardiners were gone again, taking Jane with them for a stay of several months in Town.

Elizabeth watched her sister leave with a great deal of hope. She herself had little chance of succeeding in her romantic wishes, but Jane's circumstances were different. If she could manage to see Mr. Bingley in London—not such a hard occurrence to arrange—Elizabeth was sure her older sister still had a chance at the marriage of her dreams.

But Elizabeth quickly found that, however happy she was for Jane, remaining at Longbourn without her meant a long string of dreary, uneventful days. She lived for the moments when letters arrived, hoping that each one would bring the news she so desired to hear, but Jane wrote only of her cousins and the several performances she went to with Mr. and Mrs. Gardiner. London was lovely and entertaining, she assured Elizabeth, but Elizabeth caught the lack of enthusiasm in her sister's correspondence, and her heart ached for Jane.

Georgiana's letters continued to arrive, bringing a similar mixture of excitement and pain. No matter how much Elizabeth enjoyed her new-found acquaintance with the younger girl, she also read each missive with a pounding heart, for Georgiana mentioned her brother frequently. She never again brought up his feelings for Elizabeth, though, something Elizabeth equally appreciated and noted with regret each time.

Between letters, Elizabeth spent her time learning those things she had regretted not knowing in the dark days of uncertainty when her father lay unresponsive and again when Lydia was lost, doing her best to involve her sisters. To Elizabeth's surprise, Mary picked up Italian so quickly that she was soon tutoring the other girls, and Kitty happily volunteered to share some of her tips for drawing, especially if it meant she didn't have to practice the pianoforte.

"I think we unnerve Mama," Mary remarked one afternoon when they were employed as such. "I overheard her telling Mrs. Hill that it can't be healthy for young ladies to spend so much time studying and so little on fun."

Kitty sniffed. "What's the use in chasing after fun if Lydia is gone? Besides, look where her *fun* got her. Her husband doesn't even like her that much, and she writes that they don't have enough money already. *I'm* going to marry a rich man, which means I have to be the wife such a man would want. We'll see what Lydia thinks when I'm dressed nicer than she ever is and have a carriage of my own as well!"

Kitty had been deeply hurt by Lydia's betrayal and following disappearance from her life, but Elizabeth couldn't claim the development was for the worse. Separated from Lydia's bad influence, Kitty displayed a cleverness and knack for learning that had previously been hidden, and Elizabeth's shame over dismissing her younger sister had grown steadily over the past weeks. It was a mistake she resolved not to make again, and poured a great deal of effort into coaching her younger sisters when before she would have slipped away for a walk or laughed with her father or Jane.

"I don't think Papa knows what to make of the situation either," Elizabeth replied. "He has to look outside of the family for his evening entertainment now." The realization of how poorly her beloved father treated her younger sisters had hurt as well, and there was no positive outcome to be seen there. "And Kitty, I think you'll make a lovely wife for whatever man you find." She grinned at her younger sister. "Especially if he values drawing and conversation over hearing his wife play the pianoforte."

Kitty wrinkled his nose. "Mary can come and play for us. She actually likes it, and she's gotten much better in the last month."

"I wasn't bad before," Mary protested, but there was a lack of feeling behind the complaint. She and Kitty, previously opposites in character, had started to see eye-to-eye now that they had few other options for companionship.

"Well, you've gotten better since you actually listen to critiques," Kitty stated tartly.

"Funny, I don't recall anyone taking the time to critique me before," Mary shot back. "You were all too wrapped up in chasing officers or other men."

"Have you decided what you're going to wear to the assembly tomorrow night?" Elizabeth cut in. Her younger sisters may have grown closer, but a month did not erase the habits of a lifetime.

Kitty was immediately distracted, detailing the dress and hairstyle she planned to wear with enthusiasm. Mary sniffed slightly when Kitty mentioned adding ribbons for the fourth time, but when at last Kitty had finished her recitation, Mary ventured to list an outfit as well.

"Oh no, that will never do!" Kitty cried, jumping up. "Come with me, I have just the dress that will work for you. You can't complain about ribbons if I only add a sash, can she, Lizzy?" Not waiting for an answer, Kitty grasped Mary's hand and pulled her from the room. Elizabeth was left behind, laughing. It was good to know that Kitty hadn't lost all of her enthusiasm.

The assembly itself held little appeal to Elizabeth. All of the people who had made the fall's gatherings pleasurable—Jane, Charlotte, and Mr. Darcy, a truth she hardly dared admit to herself—were absent, and she couldn't think of a single person who could truly replace any of them. Still, she was grateful that Lydia's marriage meant they were able to attend. It had to be better than another evening at home.

In the end, she enjoyed the assembly considerably more than the Netherfield Ball. Elizabeth was astonished to realize just how much stress her family's behavior had caused her at assemblies in the past. With Lydia gone, Kitty's behavior had improved inordinately—and she had taken it upon herself to make Mary dance as well, meaning the overly long and maudlin pianoforte exhibitions were also a thing of the past.

"Ah, Miss Elizabeth," Sir Lucas said, catching her arm as she passed him. "I have been meaning to talk to you, but I did not wish to interrupt your fun. You and my John looked quite dashing going through the last set. It is nice to see you stand up with some agreeable fellows, eh?"

"Thank you, Sir Lucas." Eager to stop her neighbor's certain matchmaking, and unreasonably offended at his comment about Mr. Darcy, she seized the easiest topic of distraction. "Have you heard from Charlotte lately?"

"I have indeed, and that is just what I wished to speak with you about! She has invited Maria to come and visit in just over a week, and I will be taking her to Kent myself." Moving them aside ever so slightly and lowering his voice, he went on, "She hinted that she wished to invite you as well, but Mr. Collins wouldn't hear of it. I believe Charlotte is rather upset, for you were always a great friend of hers."

Was it truly Mr. Collins that wouldn't hear of it, or had Lady Catherine been the one to oppose the idea? Knowing her cousin as she did, Elizabeth couldn't be certain, but it pained her to know that Charlotte suffered either way. Was she to lose a friend forever?

"Please let Charlotte know I would have loved to visit her, and I will send a letter with Maria. I have missed her as well, and it would have been nice to see her new home."

"Thank you, Miss Elizabeth, I will pass along your sentiments. There is one other thing I wished to ask you, and then I will let you get back to the revelries. Charlotte suggested that you may like transport to Town to visit Jane. We will go through London on the way to Kent and would be happy to take you that far, if you wish. I am sure you will make better company for Maria on the journey than I will."

Disappointment fading away, Elizabeth gave Sir Lucas a brilliant smile. "I would love that, sir. I shall have to speak with my father, of course, and write to my aunt and uncle in Town. If they are agreeable, I will be happy to take you up on your offer, and provide whatever entertainment for Maria that I can as long as I am in her company."

Sir Lucas beamed. "Splendid. We leave next Thursday, and unless you tell me differently, I shall plan on you as one of our party."

He left her, and Elizabeth turned immediately to seek out her father. A quick conversation brought about his agreement, and then she could think only of applying to her aunt. Oh, to see Jane again!

Elizabeth paused, considering. There was another person in London who might welcome the news of her arrival, should Mr. and Mrs. Gardiner approve the visit. But would it do good or harm? She took a deep breath and let it out slowly.

She would tell Georgiana if she were to come to London. And then she would let the younger girl decide what to do with the information. Yes, that plan would do quite well.

Chapter Sixteen

The sun was barely over the horizon when Elizabeth climbed into the Lucas carriage for the trip to London. Maria was half asleep, dozing with her head against the side of the carriage, and luckily Sir Lucas appeared only marginally more awake. The silence suited Elizabeth's mood, and she was happy to watch the sun rise with only her own thoughts to interrupt the peace.

The party grew livelier as they neared their noontime stop. Unfortunately for Elizabeth, the topics of conversation were far from restful.

"It is so strange to think of Lydia as married, and to Mr. Wickham, too," Maria began. "I always thought he was a favorite of yours, and he seemed to like you as well. I suppose I must have been mistaken, but then everyone has always known that Lydia is the most exciting of you all. Kitty says so too, even though she hates to admit it."

Sir Lucas said nothing to stop his daughter, although to his credit he looked distinctly uncomfortable by the end of Maria's speech.

"It is strange, I agree," Elizabeth said, striving to sound perfectly calm. "I remember when Lydia was born—and you too, for that matter," she added, giving Maria a small smile. "Both of you will always seem too young to marry to me, no matter how old we all grow. As for Mr. Wickham, I did like him. He was an interesting man and our conversations were enjoyable, but I expected nothing from him beyond friendship. Lydia did not steal him from me, if that is what you meant, and I wish them every happiness together." *And I certainly wish I believed they had any chance of being happy in their marriage,* she added silently.

"Did you know that Lydia wanted to marry him? Mama says it caught you all unaware, but I can't imagine Lydia keeping a secret like that—at least not without hints."

"Did Lydia give you any indication of what she intended?" Elizabeth returned. "No, we didn't know, and Lydia was likely aware we would have stopped her from going if she hinted at her plans, even to Kitty."

Maria frowned, likely in response to Elizabeth's first question, and for a moment it seemed like silence would return to the carriage. But the younger girl had not finished, and she soon spoke again. "Well, I'm glad for Lydia, she was so excited when she showed me her ring. It's fortunate her husband shares some of her spirit. Can you imagine being married to a bore like Mr. Darcy?"

My brother loves you, Miss Elizabeth. He believes he behaved so atrociously while in Hertfordshire that he has lost his one true chance at happiness—you. My brother loves you.

Yes, Elizabeth could imagine being married to a man like Mr. Darcy, and Maria's cavalier question hurt far more than she had expected.

Luckily, the question seemed to be a rhetorical one, and Maria continued unaware of Elizabeth's distress. "But I suppose Lydia is why Mr. Collins doesn't want you to visit Charlotte. As a clergyman, he must be careful who he associates with, and Lydia's marriage was too close to a scandal for him to accept."

Elizabeth had her own ideas on why Mr. Collins— and perhaps more to the point, Lady Catherine—did not want her to visit Kent, but she was happy to keep those to herself.

Aloud, she said only, "You might be right, Maria. I will not pretend to know Mr. Collin's reasons, but I am sure he has thought through his decision thoroughly." *And most likely does not want to host the cousin who rejected his proposal so vehemently at the home he shares with his new wife. Nor does Lady Catherine wish to see the young lady who would not bow to her will.*

"That does remind me, though, I have a letter for Charlotte. I promised her I would send one with you, since my latest message was somewhat lacking." Elizabeth fished the letter out of her bag and handed it to Maria. "And even though I cannot visit Kent with you, I appreciate that you were willing to take me as far as London." She smiled at Sir Lucas. "I am sure Jane and my aunt have numerous ideas for entertainment, but do you have any suggestions for items of interest in Town?"

As she had planned, the question sent Sir Lucas into a recitation of the many diversions that could be found in London, all seeming to lead back to St. James Palace, where he had been knighted. The dissertation lasted until the carriage stopped for lunch, and while Maria looked distinctly bored, Elizabeth greatly appreciated that Sir Lucas's soliloquy required only the minimum of input from her.

Lunch passed pleasantly, and while conversation in the carriage for the rest of the afternoon stayed away from any topics which brought Elizabeth displeasure, she was still immensely happy to see her aunt and uncle's house in Gracechurch street appear outside the carriage, with Jane and two of the younger Gardiner cousins visible in the front window. Sir Lucas and Maria were to stay the night before continuing south to Kent, but even the potential for more of Maria's impertinent questions could not pierce Elizabeth's happiness at seeing her dearest sister again.

The carriage stopped, and Elizabeth hardly waited to be helped out of the carriage. Then her cousins were there, pressed in around her and calling out greetings all at once, and Jane—*Jane!*—reaching out over their heads to clasp her hand, truly there at last. How she had missed Jane and her calming influence!

"Come in, come in," Mrs. Gardiner called from the steps, waving the new arrivals towards the door. "Ignore my young heathens, apparently the arrival of their cousin has robbed them of all manners." But she was smiling and leaned over to kiss Elizabeth's cheek as the group moved indoors. "It is good to see you, Lizzy."

"It's good to see you too, Aunt," she said. "I can't believe how much my cousins have grown since Christmas!"

"They'll grow more before you leave," Mrs. Gardiner replied. "I think I've let Henry's trousers down three times in the past month." She stepped back to let Sir Lucas and Maria pass, turning her attention to them while Elizabeth directed her focus to the cousins still clamoring for her attention.

"I have not grown that much!"

"Look at my new dress!"

"I want to grow too!"

Elizabeth laughed and bent down to pick up Alice. "I'll help you be taller," she told the toddler, who giggled.

"I growed!" Alice exclaimed, looking down from her place on Elizabeth's hip to her older siblings.

The front door opened again and Jane came in, holding Thomas by the hand. "I got to pet the horses!" he crowed, "and the driver showed me how the harnesses attach. When I grow up, I'm going to have horses just like that, and the fastest, most comfortable carriage ever!"

"It's going to be fast *and* comfortable?" Elizabeth asked with mock awe. "You'll be the envy of everyone in the kingdom."

"Not everyone!" Henry butted in. "Prinny will have a better carriage, he has to. If you're the king, you have to have the best."

Mrs. Gardiner looked over at her nieces. "Jane or Elizabeth, would you mind showing Maria up to her room? You'll all be together tonight. It may be a little crowded, but you should be comfortable."

"I'll show her," Jane volunteered immediately. "And Lizzy and I can share the larger bed, Maria, so

160

you'll have one all to yourself." They disappeared up the stairs.

"Sir Lucas, my husband was called away briefly for business, but is looking forward to seeing you soon. Until he returns, can I offer you any refreshments? Perhaps you would like to relax in the sitting room after your journey?"

"That would be wonderful," Sir Lucas said. Mrs. Gardiner gave Elizabeth a quick look, to which she replied with a shake of the head—she would not join them just yet. Sir Lucas' company was wearing on the best of occasions, and after most of a day in his company, Elizabeth wanted nothing more than a break and preferably a long conversation with Jane.

Mrs. Gardiner smiled and returned her attention to her guest. Elizabeth focused in turn on her cousins. The break from her travelling companions, she could have now. The conversation with Jane—all those things needing to be said and subtleties that could not be truly conveyed in a letter—would have to wait.

&

Sir Lucas and Maria left early the next morning for Kent. Elizabeth saw them off with only a hint of jealousy; she missed Charlotte, even if she was more than happy to avoid time with Mr. Collins and Lady Catherine.

Luckily, Mrs. Gardiner, Jane, and the Gardiner cousins distracted Elizabeth quickly, dragging her out for walks in the nearby parks, stopping at sweet shops, and regaling her with tales of Jane's time in London. Before she knew it, two days had passed with no time to regret her exclusion from Charlotte's new home.

On the third morning of Elizabeth's visit, she and Jane had just settled themselves in the sitting room—Jane helping their cousin Priscilla with embroidery stitches and Elizabeth reluctantly attending to her own needlework—when there was a commotion at the front door. A moment later, the Gardiner's maid appeared.

"Miss Bennet and Miss Elizabeth, you have visitors."

Jane and Elizabeth frowned at each other. Visitors? They knew almost no one in Town. "Who is it?" Elizabeth asked.

"Gentlemen, miss. A Mr. Bingley and a Mr. Darcy."

Jane's face blanched white, and Elizabeth felt her own heart kick into overdrive, blood pounding in her ears.

"Show them in, thank you. Prissy, run up and let your mother know that we have guests," Jane said, sounding far calmer than Elizabeth knew she felt.

Prissy left the room, and Elizabeth turned to her sister. Jane was subtly avoiding her gaze, cheeks pinker than they had been a moment ago, hands twisting in her skirts. If Elizabeth was caught off guard by the announcement, she could only image Jane's surprise. At least Elizabeth could guess how the visit had come about.

Then the gentlemen were at the door, and even in the rush of emotions that swarmed over Elizabeth at Darcy's presence, she could not tear her eyes from Jane. As soon as the door opened, her sister had released the death grip on her skirt and straightened her shoulders, but Elizabeth could still see where the fabric had been crushed. Jane smiled, her eyes on Bingley, but there was hesitation on her face instead of the pure joy that used to shine upon his arrival. Still, she was smiling, and he was there. Surely that was better than the long days after he had left Netherfield, when Jane had hardly spoken, let alone smiled.

"Mr. Bingley, Mr. Darcy," Jane said, dipping a curtsey for their guests.

Elizabeth followed suit, turning her eyes to the gentlemen for the first time, and found that Mr. Darcy seemed to be watching Jane as well. Then he glanced over and his eyes caught hers. Elizabeth felt her face flush at the mixed rush of emotions that his presence conjured up. Now that he stood in front of her, she found it hard to accept Georgiana's words as truth—how *could* they be, when they had last parted with such bitter words? And so much had occurred since those words were spoken. She had changed many of her opinions in that time; it was reasonable to believe he may have reconsidered as well.

Luckily for Elizabeth, the door behind Darcy and Bingley opened and Mrs. Gardiner entered. Jane performed introductions, complete with several uncharacteristic pauses and blushes. Elizabeth watched her aunt and Mr. Darcy carefully, but both acted as if the other was a complete stranger. The gentlemen were invited to sit, and within only a few minutes Jane and Bingley were seated in adjacent chairs, both seeming rather embarrassed but steadily conversing nonetheless.

Elizabeth did not find herself in such a happy situation. She, Mr. Darcy, and Mrs. Gardiner had seated themselves slightly away from Jane and Mr. Bingley, due in large part to the arrangement of chairs in the room. Elizabeth, usually happy to talk if only to amuse herself, found herself tongue-tied, and so they passed several minutes of long pauses and stilted conversation.

Finally, Mrs. Gardiner turned to Darcy. "My nieces have told me that you are from Derbyshire, and in fact grew up at Pemberley. Is that the truth?"

Mr. Darcy answered that it was, face absolutely expressionless. Had they discussed this when he came to arrange Lydia's marriage? Elizabeth had no way to tell.

Mrs. Gardiner's smile grew. "I spent my girlhood in Lambton, only five miles from Pemberley, and I often think of the area. Have you been back recently?"

Darcy actually smiled. "I was able to visit this winter, but I have not spent as much time there as I would like in recent years."

"You can understand how much I miss it, then," Mrs. Gardiner said with a rueful smile. "My husband has promised me a visit to see old friends, but his business makes it hard for him to get away. I have had to content myself with the anticipation of the trip." She turned to Elizabeth. "If we ever make the journey, you shall have to go with us, Lizzy. I may not be much of a walker anymore, but in my girlhood I loved rambling over the hills. The views are unlike anything you have in Hertfordshire."

Much to her mortification, Elizabeth felt herself blush. Her aunt meant well, but the comment seemed to suggest too much in front of Mr. Darcy. What would he think of her invading his home?

"It is beautiful, but also wilder than anything in the south of England," Darcy said, seeming not to notice Elizabeth's confusion. "I find it better for riding than walking, and it is not a good place to be alone if you are unfamiliar with the landscape. I have heard far too many stories of people becoming lost, and the terrain is unforgiving after dark."

The words felt like a punch to Elizabeth's stomach. He had expressed his distaste for her walks very clearly in Hertfordshire, scolded her for daring to venture out alone in a place she had known her entire life. She could only imagine his reaction if they were to cross paths in Derbyshire—would he throw her over his horse and cart her back to civilization should she dare to walk alone? Or would he leave her to her fate, washing his hands of a woman so obviously lacking in what he would call common sense? Oh, how fickle she was! The mere thought of his dismissal filled her with regret when she had once valued her own independence over anything else, even as she wanted to snap that she could take care of herself.

But Darcy had not finished. He looked directly at her for the first time in several minutes. "If you visit Lambton with your aunt when I am in residence, I would be most willing to show you some of the better walks, and if I am not present my steward would do the same. I find they are more enjoyable when you know the history of the landscape, and you would be able to enjoy the sights without fear of becoming lost."

Somehow, she managed to reply, although Elizabeth could not have said what that response was. Vaguely, she was aware of the conversation turning to a discussion of the seasons in Derbyshire. For herself, though, she could only sit in silence and contemplate how much easier life had been when she had considered herself the cleverest judge of character in all of Hertfordshire. It was uncomfortable to realize how poorly she had judged Mr. Darcy—and even worse to think how wrong she might still be about herself.

Chapter Seventeen

By some miraculous force of will, Elizabeth found it possible to conceal her trepidation of calling on Darcy House the following morning. Had Jane been focused on her sister, Elizabeth knew she never would have succeeded, but Jane's thoughts had clearly stayed with a blond-haired gentleman long after he physically departed from Gracechurch Street.

Since Mr. Darcy had invited them to call on his sister before the gentlemen left and Mr. Bingley had promptly expressed his delight at the idea, Jane could think of no reason not to make the call—and Elizabeth could not think of how to reject it without telling Jane just how much her feelings had changed since December. Mrs. Gardiner had stayed home with Alice, who was feeling sick, and so Elizabeth was able to set off on a visit she didn't want to make without anyone questioning her uncharacteristic low spirits.

At least it had to be better than calling on Miss Bingley and Mrs. Hurst, Elizabeth reasoned with herself as the carriage made its way towards Grosvenor Square. There, she knew the visit would turn unpleasant for both herself and Jane in one way or another. At Darcy House, there was a chance that Jane would enjoy the experience. As for her own feelings about the place, Elizabeth could not entirely name how she felt, and she was not inclined to dwell on the matter at length. Instead, she focused on the fact that she would finally meet Georgiana Darcy, and did her best to avoid all thought of the girl's brother.

And yet for the entire way across town, Elizabeth debated opening her heart to her sister. It seemed impossible, though. If she could not whisper the truth in the dark of their bedroom, how could it be told in broad daylight—and on the way to see the man himself, no less? Then they were there, pulling up before a regal house at least twice the size of her aunt and uncle's.

"Oh my," Jane said faintly, which summed up Elizabeth's feelings as well. No wonder Darcy had seemed unimpressed with Longbourn and the Meryton Assembly Hall, if this was where he called home—no, *one* of the places he called home.

"I'm sure you'll get used to it, Jane," Elizabeth said. "Just think, when you marry Mr. Bingley you'll come here for dinner so often you'll hardly notice the splendor."

"I don't think that is possible!" Jane exclaimed, her cheeks turning pink. "And you shouldn't speak so, I have no such expectations."

"Yes, and we spoke of Mr. Bingley's goodness all morning merely as a way to pass the time," Elizabeth replied.

The carriage door opened, and Jane could only throw a disapproving look in Elizabeth's direction before she exited. The sisters made their way to the front door, and with each step Elizabeth became more aware of her year-old dress and simple hairstyle. The second she realized her thoughts, she frowned; Lizzy Bennet had always valued who someone was more than how they looked, and she would not let an imposing house in Grosvenor Square take that from her.

The door opened at their knock, and Elizabeth swallowed back the last of her nerves. "Miss Bennet and Miss Elizabeth Bennet to see Miss Darcy."

The footman took their cards and ushered them into the entry hall with only a hint of disapproval. "If you will wait here, I will see if Miss Darcy is at home this morning."

Elizabeth tried not to gape at the entry hall as they waited, contenting herself by sharing one incredulous, disbelieving look with Jane before fixing a polite smile on her face and doing her best to ignore her suddenly sweaty palms. With no context, she would have assumed they stood in Carlton House, the Prince Regent's residence.

The doorman returned with quick steps. "Right this way if you please, ladies." Was she mistaken, or did he seem surprised at their admittance? If so, Elizabeth supposed she couldn't rightly blame him.

They were shown up the stairs and into an elegant, but welcoming drawing room. The two ladies within—Elizabeth guessed immediately they were Georgiana and her companion—stood upon their entrance, but both remained silent even after the footman had departed and all four ladies had curtseyed to one another. Georgiana seemed eager to avoid meeting their eyes for as long as she could, and two spots of color highlighted her pale cheeks.

Elizabeth glanced around the room and was surprised not to find Mr. Darcy. According to the rules of society, she and Jane could not interact with Georgiana until properly introduced, and as Georgiana's brother and guardian, that duty should have fallen to Mr. Darcy. In his absence, the two parties could only stare at each other while Elizabeth tried to decide if exchanging letters with Georgiana had freed her from this traditional meeting. No wonder Georgiana looked so distressed!

Recalling the younger girl's declaration of shyness and uncertainty in her first letter, Elizabeth took pity on her hostess and made up her mind. She stepped further into the room and smiled. "Good morning ladies. I am Miss Elizabeth Bennet, and this is my sister, Miss Jane Bennet. I presume you are Miss Darcy," she said with an encouraging smile, for Georgiana had looked up during her speech.

"I am," the girl replied in a voice barely above a whisper. "This is my companion, Mrs. Annesley. Please, be seated."

As Jane and Elizabeth settled themselves on a settee across from the other ladies, Elizabeth had to wonder at the extent of Georgiana's shyness, especially since it differed so strongly from the lively girl she had come to know through letters. Did her reticence only occur in person? If not, Elizabeth could hardly imagine the strength of conviction it must have required to pen such a personal letter to a stranger. What sentiment had Mr. Darcy expressed that possessed Georgiana to pick up that pen?

The party would have lapsed into silence again, with Elizabeth too agitated and uncertain to focus her energy on making conversation, but Jane leaned forward with her friendliest smile. "That is a beautiful instrument, Miss Darcy," she said, indicating the pianoforte sitting next to a window. "Do you enjoy playing?"

She had found the magic topic, as Elizabeth should have known. "Oh, very much," Georgiana replied with considerably less reserve. "It was a surprise from my brother this past autumn, and I think it is the most beautiful pianoforte I have ever seen, even more so than my instrument at Pemberley. Of course, it was far more than I deserved, but I do delight in playing on such an instrument."

Elizabeth noted the time frame and wondered if Mr. Darcy had purchased the pianoforte to distract his little sister from Mr. Wickham and the heartache he had caused. Aloud, she said, "Its beauty must prove beneficial as well. Even I, who am so lax in my playing, could be induced to practice on such an instrument."

"I am sure you do not do justice to your skill," Georgiana returned at once, meeting Elizabeth's gaze with earnest eyes.

Elizabeth laughed. "I would apply to Jane for backup, but she can say no ill of anyone. I have heard of your proficiency from numerous parties, and I suffer no delusions over my own skill. I am competent at best."

Georgiana opened her mouth, no doubt to make another rebuttal, but just then the door swung open and Mr. Darcy entered the room. "Good day, Miss Bennet, Miss Elizabeth," he said with a slight bow.

They rose and curtseyed.

"I apologize I was not present to make introductions," Darcy continued. "I was delayed with business and did not return home as early as I had hoped." He looked directly at Elizabeth as he spoke, and she felt compelled to respond.

"It seems that a beautiful instrument does wonders in making acquaintances out of strangers," she said. The words rang false; Georgiana had ceased to be a stranger months ago, but as far as the world—and more importantly, Jane—was aware, they were true. To cover her confusion, Elizabeth continued, "Since you are here now, perhaps you can settle a disagreement, for I know you to be an honest man. Miss Darcy seems convinced that my skills on the pianoforte far exceed reality, and Jane would tell me I played beautifully even if I missed half of the notes. How would you rate my playing, Mr. Darcy?"

She had spoken without considering the audience, and regretted the comment immediately upon catching sight of Georgiana's face. It was lit with anticipation, and the girl's eyes darted back and forth between her brother and Elizabeth.

Elizabeth frowned at her, but could not help herself from glancing at Darcy as well. Then she was forced to bite back a laugh, hastily turning it into a cough. He had directed the exact same sort of frown at Georgiana as the one she wore herself.

"Miss Elizabeth, you put me in an undesirable position," Mr. Darcy said, looking away from his sister. "The answer that I know you want from me is that I find your playing tolerable, but nothing more. I cannot give that answer in good faith, for I have enjoyed your playing far too much to demean it in such a fashion. However, if I say you are quite the proficient, you will not believe me and be vexed, for you applied specifically to my honesty. I can only say that you are not as technically skilled as Georgiana, who has studied music extensively, but you bring a great deal of joy to your playing, which makes the music more enjoyable than skill alone would allow."

Jane laughed gleefully. "How will you answer that, Lizzy?"

Elizabeth forced herself to laugh as well, hoping it would cover the confusion caused by his answer. Must she be perpetually confused in his presence? "I cede the point, Mr. Darcy, if only because I cannot think of a retort that would rival yours for eloquence."

"You admit defeat, Miss Elizabeth?" Mr. Darcy asked.

"Is it defeat to accept that you gave your honest opinion when that is what I asked of you? I still disagree with you, but I am vain enough to prefer that the lowest opinion of myself should be my own."

Acutely aware that Jane, Georgiana, and Mrs. Annesley were all watching the exchange with interest, Elizabeth turned decisively back to her hostess. "Do you enjoy attending musical performances as well as playing, Miss Darcy?"

"I adore the opera," Georgiana replied, although her voice remained quiet and almost timid. "We have a box, and Fitzwilliam takes me at least once a month when he is in Town."

She should not be distracted by his given name. She *would* not be distracted.

But it was no use to decide that after the fact, for Georgiana had continued speaking and Elizabeth could only guess what had been said. Luckily, Jane leaned forward and began to discuss the shows she had seen with Mr. and Mrs. Gardiner earlier in the season.

"I am glad there are people who enjoy performing," Jane added, once the performances had been discussed and compared. "I could never exhibit in front of so many people, but I do love being part of the crowd."

Georgiana nodded emphatically. "Oh, I feel exactly the same. I used to wonder what it would feel like to stand under the bright lights on the stage, but I know I would freeze up and completely forget everything I had rehearsed. I get nervous just imaging all those eyes on me."

Jane glanced at Elizabeth, a smile flickering in the corners of her mouth, and Elizabeth immediately guessed what she was thinking. Forgetting for a moment that she was not back in Hertfordshire with longtime acquaintances, Elizabeth glared at her sister.

Jane ignored her. "My sister," she said to Georgiana, "used to make all of us perform sketches that she wrote. Of course, *she* always played the daring heroine who saved us all from unimaginable danger."

Georgiana giggled, and Mr. Darcy made a choked sound. Elizabeth shot him accusatory look. "I believe I was eight at the time, Mr. Darcy. Surely you—" she stopped short. Had Mr. Wickham been Darcy's playmate at the age of eight? Would speaking of childish escapades bring him to mind for both of the Darcy siblings?

Well, it was too late to stop now. "Surely *everyone* is silly in some way at the age of eight," Elizabeth continued. "At least I did not try to hide a calf in my room as Lydia when *she* was eight."

"My goodness, how did she do that?" Georgiana asked. "And why?"

A commotion in the entryway below interrupted Elizabeth's planned answer. Darcy went to the window. "Ah. I wondered when Bingley would be here."

Voices floated up the stairs, including one that was all too familiar. Before realizing what she was doing, Elizabeth exchanged an exasperated look with Georgiana. Caroline Bingley had arrived with her brother.

The lady sailed several feet into the room before she noticed Jane and Elizabeth, and it was immediately clear that Mr. Bingley had not told his sister who else would be present. Obviously taken aback, it took Caroline several seconds to arrange her face into something resembling a smile. "Miss Bennet! What a pleasant surprise. And Miss Eliza." Apparently, Caroline could not bring herself to call Elizabeth's presence anything socially acceptable, for she hesitated a moment longer and then continued over to Georgiana.

"Miss Darcy! How good it is to see you again. And how kind of you to welcome new acquaintances into your home, especially those not in your social sphere."

From the corner of her eye, Elizabeth saw Darcy's attention jerk towards Caroline, mouth opening as if he would challenge her statement.

Georgiana, however, was not in need of assistance. "But they are not new acquaintances, Miss Bingley," she said quietly, but in a tone that left no room for doubt. "I made Miss Elizabeth's acquaintance nearly four months ago, and I am pleased to consider her a friend. And of course Miss Bennet is delightful company. They are better company than many of those *in my sphere*."

Mr. Bingley, who had entered behind his sister and gone directly to Jane's side, beamed at Georgiana. "You are absolutely correct, Miss Darcy. I find the present company delightful. Do you not agree, Caroline?"

Miss Bingley seemed to be fighting the urge to throw a fit. "Delightful," she repeated in a brittle tone.

"Georgiana, shall we call for tea?" Mr. Darcy asked. Was Elizabeth imagining it, or was his voice strained?

"Oh!" the girl jumped. "Yes, yes, of course."

Darcy settled himself in a chair closer to the window than to the rest of the group, and as Bingley began a conversation with Jane, Elizabeth found herself staring across the room at Caroline Bingley. The other woman was watching Mr. Darcy with an air of incredulous dismay.

Since she kept glancing towards the man as well, Elizabeth was left with the uncomfortable thought that she had a great deal more sympathy for the Caroline Bingley than she'd ever imagined possible during their time in Hertfordshire. Oh, how much simpler life had been when she could hate them both!

Chapter Eighteen

Had the person in question been anyone other than
Caroline Bingley, Elizabeth may have maintained her
new-found sympathy indefinitely. Since it *was*
Caroline, however, the sentiment lasted only three
days, and two of those days consisted of no
interaction between the ladies. In fact, Jane and
Elizabeth heard nothing at all from the Darcys or
Bingleys, male or female, for a day and a half after
the morning call to Darcy House.

Having met and talked directly with Mr. Bingley
twice now, Jane bore the silence with a true smile on
her face, entertaining her young cousins with even
more sweetness than before. No matter what had
happened in the past, no one watching could doubt
that Mr. Bingley was still very much enamored with
the eldest Bennet sister.

For Elizabeth, the silence was torture. She refused
to put a name on her feelings for Mr. Darcy, but that
did not stop her from knowing that he was perhaps

the only man she would ever truly want to marry. At Longbourn, where there had been no expectation of interaction, the regret was manageable. It was different in Town. He knew she was here and had visited before—was it unreasonable to expect him again? Was it politeness that has brought him to Gracechurch Street? A show of support for Bingley, with no interests of his own involved? And what was she to make of his actions when they *had* met? As a result, her own interactions with her cousins were better described as distracted than sweet.

Luckily for Elizabeth's sanity, an invitation arrived for the Bennet sisters just after luncheon on the second day, inviting them to a walking party in Hyde Park the following afternoon.

"You'll like that, Lizzy," Jane said once the invitation had been read. "I know you've missed your walks while you've been here."

"You'll like it as long as a certain young gentleman is there to escort you," Elizabeth teased.

"And what about the gentleman who will be escorting you?" Jane asked in return. "I believe you will like that as well."

Elizabeth felt herself flush. "I don't know who you mean," she replied, hoping her voice sounded as resolute as she meant for it to be. "Mr. Bingley will see no one but you, Mr. Hurst will escort his wife—if he deigns to attend the outing—and Miss Bingley will commandeer Mr. Darcy's attention. What gentleman do you propose as my escort?"

"Perhaps the one who has proposed in another fashion?" Jane asked in a barely-audible voice. "I know you believe me blind to the world when Mr. Bingley is present, but I saw how he reacted to Miss Bingley on Friday—and how he reacted to you, as well." Elizabeth knew her sister did not mean Mr. Bingley when she said *he*.

"Nonsense. If Mr. Darcy does not wish to walk with Miss Bingley, then he will attend to Georgiana."

"Georgiana," Jane repeated slowly. "That is another question I have for you, sister dear. She called you a friend yesterday, which I can scarcely believe is the outcome of a single letter. Miss Darcy does not seem the type to exaggerate, either, even when pressed. And Mr. Darcy did not seem surprised by the statement. I am sure you noticed his reaction to Miss Bingley's comment?"

"That does not seem to be much of a question," Elizabeth answered evasively.

"You know what I mean and are choosing to not understand. How frequently have you and, ah, *Georgiana* corresponded since her first letter arrived?"

Elizabeth studied her sister steadily for a moment, wondering if she had misjudged Jane as well. She had never known the older girl to speak in such a direct fashion. "Perhaps once a week," she replied, wondering what Jane's response would be.

"And is her brother aware of this fact?"

"I have reason to believe he is, although I could not say to what extent."

The door to the sitting room opened and the Gardiner children ran in, released from their daily lessons. Jane continued to watch Elizabeth for a moment, then gave a small smile and turned to her cousins.

Yes, she had definitely underestimated Jane.

&

Nothing more of consequence had passed between the sisters by the time they met the rest of the party the following afternoon. The others arrived all together, coming as they were from the nearby Grosvenor Square. As Elizabeth had predicted, Caroline Bingley held Mr. Darcy's arm in a way that bordered on clinging. Georgiana held his other arm, and Elizabeth couldn't help but smile at how Georgiana's warm, if shy, greeting contrasted with Miss Bingley's cool acknowledgement. The man himself was cordial, but she barely dared to meet his eyes. Never before had she felt so off-balance, and Elizabeth was sure her behavior would betray her feelings.

Once pleasantries had been exchanged, the group started off down one of the wider lanes. Mr. Hurst had indeed joined the party, and Louisa Hurst walked with her husband. Jane and Mr. Bingley walked together, which left Mr. Darcy's group of three and Elizabeth on her own.

Recognizing the situation, Mr. Darcy stopped, frowning. Before he could say anything, however, Miss Bingley gave a showy laugh.

"Oh dear, Miss Eliza, we have quite the unfortunate ratio of gentlemen to ladies. It is a shame there are no officers here to escort you." She paused long enough to give a clearly insincere smile, then continued. "What was the name of your favorite? Oh yes, Mr. Wickham! I was most surprised to hear that your sister had married him, for he seemed to favor you as well. I do hope there are no hard feelings between you and the new Mrs. Wickham. I should hate it dreadfully if Louisa and I quarreled over a man."

At the mention of Mr. Wickham, Darcy's face had frozen and Georgiana's drained of all color. Luckily, Caroline was only watching Elizabeth, who had been on guard from the second Miss Bingley began to talk.

"I wish Lydia and Mr. Wickham every happiness in their marriage," Elizabeth replied calmly. It was true, she thought wryly to herself—she just didn't think it was likely. "It would be unfortunate if Mr.

Wickham had engaged my emotions, so I will count myself lucky that he did not. I enjoyed his conversation when we met in Hertfordshire, but we said goodbye with no great sorrow."

Caroline's smile took on an even more bitter edge. "I'm surprised you can still wish her well after how she behaved. Of course, it may just be gossip, but the idea has to come from somewhere." She glanced at Georgiana, then gave Mr. Darcy a simpering smile before fixing her gaze back on Elizabeth. "I should hate to distress Miss Darcy with unpleasant truths, and in any case, it seems that the problem is solved now. But it must be dreadful knowing that your sister ran off with a man and your uncle had to pay him before he would marry her! It certainly reflects poorly on you and your other sisters, knowing that one of you behaved as no young lady should."

"Lydia is very young," Elizabeth said, watching Georgiana from the corner of her eye. The other girl appeared to be composed, but the statement had to have hurt her more than it had affected Elizabeth herself. Yes, Elizabeth would have happily strangled Lydia for behaving the way she had, but she would never say such a thing in front of Georgiana. Instead, she continued as if they were discussing Darcy's sister, not her own. "You are correct that she did not behave in the best manner, but who has not made a mistake at one time or another? I am glad the situation was remedied, and as for wishing her well, how can I not? She is my sister, and I am not so

185

shallow as to love her only in pleasant times."
Elizabeth gave a sharp-edged smile of her own. "As
you pointed out, you also have a sister, Miss Bingley.
I am sure you understand."

Turning to Georgiana, Elizabeth smiled honestly.
"Shall we walk, Miss Darcy? I fear we will lose the
others if we do not start after them soon."

Still blank-faced, Georgiana stepped away from
her brother and allowed Elizabeth to link arms with
her, and they walked off down the path in a manner
that said both were completely at ease. The moment
she touched the younger girl, however, Elizabeth
became acutely aware that her companion was
trembling. "Are you alright?" she murmured, once
they had taken several steps away from Caroline and
put her out of hearing range.

"I hate her," Georgiana whispered back, still
looking straight ahead. "She praises me
continuously; everything I do is amazing, but if she
paid any attention to what I'm really like or knew
what I did, she'd despise me just like she does your
sister. And then she acts like I won't notice when she
treats everyone else horribly, at least as long as my
brother isn't there to see her behavior."

"Do you spend much time around her?" Elizabeth
asked in an undertone.

"More than I would like," Georgiana said. "In all
honesty, though, I think Fitzwilliam tries to arrange

situations so I do not have to entertain her and Mrs. Hurst whenever he can manage it without being rude, and I very rarely go to visit them. I'm not out, you see, and Miss Bingley loves to hold parties that are not suitable for a girl of my age." She said the last phrase in such a way that Elizabeth understood it to be a long-standing excuse that allowed Georgiana to escape events where she would be miserable.

"Your brother is appearing smarter by the minute," Elizabeth said wryly, realizing only after she spoke that praising Mr. Darcy to Georgiana was likely to start a conversation she did not want to have. Thinking quickly, she added, "Come, let us change the subject before we are accused of being too serious on such a beautiful day. Can you guess what my cousin Henry said when I told him where we were going today?"

From the look on Georgiana's face, she was not fooled by Elizabeth's tactic, but allowed the subject to be changed without comment. They kept up a steady stream of conversation for the next quarter-hour, never touching on anything too personal or serious, until the party stopped to watch several young men racing horses down Rotten Row.

Apparently feeling in control after monopolizing Mr. Darcy for the entirety of the outing thus far, Caroline released him and drifted over to join Jane's conversation with Mrs. Hurst. As the rest of the party rearranged itself in a similar manner, Elizabeth found herself standing next to Mr. Darcy.

After a lengthy pause, during which both of them made a greater study of the horses than the animals deserved, Darcy spoke. "Did you mean what you said?" he asked, still not looking directly at her.

"I make a practice of telling the truth as I believe it, even when I would be better served holding my tongue," Elizabeth replied. "To which comment are you referring, precisely?"

"What you said to Miss Bingley, about Mr. Wickham and," he hesitated, "and your feelings on your sister's marriage."

Elizabeth frowned, confused by both the question and its inherent meaning. "Did you doubt it? I thought I made my feelings on the matter clear when I wrote Georgiana, and I know that a great deal of the contents were passed along to you. I assumed you had read all."

To her surprise, he looked flustered by the response. "I will not pretend to misunderstand you. Georgiana did bring me your letter, but since I was not the intended recipient, I did my best to read only the parts necessary to understand the situation. Georgiana was, understandably, most upset and it took time to make sense of what she said."

Elizabeth tried to imagine the scene. Had he known of his sister's letter, or was it a complete surprise when she handed over a missive signed by the woman that had rejected him not a month previously? And—if Georgiana's original letter contained the truth of the matter—had it hurt him? *That* was something she did not want to imagine.

Realizing she had not responded, Lizzy reigned in her thoughts. "I suppose I gave a very different impression when we last spoke at Netherfield. In retrospect, I cannot blame you for questioning me."

"And in fairness, *I* cannot blame *you* for misunderstanding the situation when I offered no alternative explanation. You would not be the first person to…" Darcy added, almost under his breath.

Elizabeth waited, but he did not seem inclined to finish the thought. "To 'have been told falsehoods by a man with a sweet voice and a jealous heart?'" she quoted, feeling her face flush as she recalled how Georgiana had finished that line in her letter. *My brother loves you.*

Darcy glanced up. "Precisely. Although I would not have expected such a phrasing from you." He frowned, eyes darting past Elizabeth to the rest of the group.

"You are correct. I am quoting, and I believe you have guessed the original author."

He was frowning in earnest now. "She told you. I guessed as much, although I did not ask her outright. I should be furious with her, but I cannot be. She has improved since last fall; perhaps a female confidante was what she needed. And you have told…?"

"No one," Elizabeth replied readily. "As I believe my letter said, I tried to impart warning to my sisters without revealing anything, but the attempt was clearly in vain."

"My, you look so serious!" Caroline Bingley exclaimed, coming up behind the pair. Elizabeth suddenly realized that, in their attempt to keep the conversation inaudible to anyone else, she and Mr. Darcy had moved closer together than society considered acceptable. "Surely you are not arguing again," Caroline continued. "Did your mother not tell you that men prefer agreeable young ladies, Eliza? Whatever can you be discussing that requires such a frown?"

"We were speaking of sisters," Elizabeth said, shifting so she could see the rest of the party. Jane and Mr. Bingley still stood side-by-side, conversing with Mr. and Mrs. Hurst. Georgiana was between the two parties, watching them intently, but she would know what Elizabeth meant and not take offense.

"Yes, you should take whatever advice that Mr. Darcy can give you. You would do well to coach your second youngest sister—what is her name? —to behave more like Georgiana. Oh, my!" Caroline widened her eyes at something over Elizabeth's shoulder, and Elizabeth swung around to see what had caught her attention.

Two horses were racing down Rotten Row, as they had been for much of the afternoon, but in this case only one horse was under control. The pair drew nearer with alacrity, both riders shouting. Just as they reached Elizabeth's group, one horse slowed and stopped, blowing heavily but showing signs of calming down. The other one veered sideways, neck arched as it fought the rider for control of the bit.

Moving backwards, Elizabeth collided with Miss Bingley. "Oh dear!" the other woman exclaimed, hands coming up to Elizabeth's back. Rather than stepping aside so Elizabeth could move, however, Caroline stayed put. The horse skittered closer, and Elizabeth noticed the whites of its eyes, vivid against the dark skin surrounding them. Then she was acutely aware of pressure on her back thrusting her into the lane. She took an unwilling step forward, still resisting, and tripped on a loose stone at the edge of the Row.

Elizabeth heard the huffing of the horse's breath, a gasp from behind her, and a shriek. Then she was falling.

Chapter Nineteen

If her father's collapse had caused the world to slow down and fade, being pushed towards an unruly horse did the opposite. Elizabeth was aware of everything. The way the stone of the path changed color when the horse's shadow crossed it. The rustling of her dress. Bingley's shout as the others realized what was happening. A nick on the horse's left hoof that made a white mark against the black. The sensation of falling, and how the wind it created blew her hair back from her face.

Then she was jerked back, and her attention snapped to the arm tightening around her middle, the way her head snapped forward with the motion. Small rocks hit her legs as the rider finally managed to pull the blowing horse to a stop, hooves kicking up rocks as they slid on the lane. One flying rock caught the back of her hand, making it sting. There were more voices, shouting over each other now. And directly behind her, the ragged breathing and rapid heartbeat of the man whose body was pressed against her from shoulder to thigh.

And despite the difference in her reaction, Elizabeth knew that was the similarity to the Netherfield Ball. When her knees forgot how to work, when the world turned sideways, he was there, something strong and steady and warm to crash into. In that moment, Elizabeth knew that she was in love with Mr. Darcy—that she had been for a long time, and to call it anything else was insanity. It wasn't just the lack of an advantageous marriage that she had been regretting, or even a husband that she could respect.

My brother loves you, Miss Elizabeth. She, who had laughed at men for her entire life, had not truly understood the significance of that statement until now.

Strangely, the realization gave her the strength to find her own feet and step away from him—or at least try to, for he kept one arm firmly locked around her midsection. Turning her head, Elizabeth half wondered if she could find a way to communicate her sentiments to the man in question. At that moment, there was no question in her mind that he would understand her. For him to feel differently was unthinkable.

But he wasn't looking at her. Darcy's gaze was fixed unwaveringly on Caroline Bingley, and he wore an expression she had seen only once before: when Mr. Collins had threatened her in Longbourn's garden.

The rider was speaking—apologizing, Elizabeth thought as she forced her attention away from Darcy and the heat of his body down her back. Bingley and Hurst had hurried over and both addressed the man. In typical fashion, Bingley expressed concern for both horse and rider while Mr. Hurst chastised. The man met Elizabeth's eyes and repeated an apology, his gaze darting nervously to Darcy and back again as if he could feel the anger radiating from the other man. Then the horse snorted, tossing its head, and the rider urged him away from the group before any more harm could be done.

Beginning to grow uncomfortable, Elizabeth reached up and touched the arm that still encircled her. Mr. Darcy jumped as if the contact sent a shock through him, and this time when she stepped away he released her. He turned abruptly away from Caroline, focusing his intense gaze on Elizabeth instead. "Are you well?" he asked.

Elizabeth paused, taking a moment to assess her condition now that she could think clearly—or at least somewhat clearly, as she was still too aware of how cold her back now felt. "I am," she replied. Feeling enough of her natural humor return to appreciate the irony of her situation, she added quietly, "Or at least, I am well in body. In mind, my independent nature is disturbed by how many times I have required such a rescue in recent months. You must think me quite the damsel in distress, a description I have always abhorred."

Darcy's frown deepened, but he seemed contemplative rather than angry. "For all that your independence creates opportunities for mishaps, I cannot think of you in such a way. If I am correct in assuming which situations you are referencing, then I do not hesitate to lay the blame for each on reasons outside your control, and I am sure you could have handled them alone if required."

Unintentionally, Elizabeth's eyes fell to long scuffs left by the horse's hooves, ending less than three feet from where she stood. The severity of what could have happened settled over her like a heavy cloak, and she dug the fingernails of her right hand into her palm to refocus herself. Looking back up, she found Darcy staring at the hoof marks as well.

"Perhaps," Elizabeth replied, even more quietly now. "But neither of us can see what might have been."

"Lizzy! Your hand!" Jane exclaimed, and the strange tension stretching between Darcy and Elizabeth was broken.

"Oh, goodness, you're bleeding," Georgiana said, taking a step forward in concern and then hesitating as if unsure how to react.

Elizabeth lifted her hand to inspect it better. She was indeed bleeding—the rock must have opened a cut when it struck—and the blood had flowed from just below her wrist down across the back of her left hand. The cut did not look severe, though, and thanks to the adrenaline, she scarcely felt the pain.

"Here," Jane said, holding out a lace-edged handkerchief.

Elizabeth pulled back automatically. "Jane, I can't use that! Prissy just gave it to you, and I'll stain it."

"Do you mean to bleed on your skirts instead?" Jane asked, pressing the handkerchief closer. "You are hurt; Prissy will understand."

"Miss Elizabeth," Darcy said, a request in his voice. She turned towards him, making sure to keep her now-dripping hand away from her body, and saw that he was offering a plain handkerchief, folded into a long strip. "May I?" he asked, gesturing towards her hand, and after a moment's hesitation she held out the offending appendage.

Darcy's fingers closed around her wrist and Elizabeth had to bite her lip to keep from gasping as the touch sent a shock through her body. He deftly wiped the blood from the back of her hand, then wrapped the cloth around the injury and tucked in the end, creating a tidy bandage that she could keep secure by closing her hand into a fist.

The work had brought him quite close, and their eyes met as he looked up from her hand. Elizabeth's breath caught; Darcy's pupils dilated. For a moment they both froze, staring at each other. Then Darcy stepped back and inclined his head towards Jane. "Is this alternative acceptable, Miss Bennet?"

"It is," Jane replied, a faint look of astonishment on her face. Then she appeared to collect herself. "I believe Lizzy over-exaggerated the importance of my handkerchief, but I thank you all the same."

"For goodness' sake, it is a piece of cloth!" Miss Bingley burst out. "The wound hardly needed tending, and Miss Eliza has shown such little care for her gowns she could have torn a strip from her hem to achieve the same result."

Heat rushed to Elizabeth's face and down her spine as anger flooded through her. "Jane, perhaps we should return home," she said with forced calm. "I would hate to inconvenience Miss Bingley any more than I have already, and I am not feeling equal to any more mishaps today." She curtseyed to Bingley and the Hursts, then turned and offered the same gesture to Darcy and Georgiana. Georgiana returned the curtsey, concern on her face. Darcy appeared to be fighting back fury.

"You must allow us to give you a ride back to your aunt and uncle's house," Mr. Bingley said.

To Elizabeth's immense surprise, it was Mrs. Hurst who echoed the idea. "Yes, I would be happy to accompany you in our carriage. I am amazed at your composure, Elizabeth. I surely would have gone into hysterics by now."

Elizabeth, intimately acquainted with her mother's fits of nerves, found them nothing more than a waste of time and energy, but she also recognized that Mrs. Hurst—for once—seemed to genuinely mean what she said. "Thank you for your concern, Mrs. Hurst. I am not prone to hysterics, but I confess that I still feel as though I am in shock." She glanced at Jane for confirmation, then smiled at Mr. Bingley. "We would be glad to accept your offer of a ride."

"Oh, you must call me Louisa," Mrs. Hurst said, bustling over and taking Elizabeth's uninjured arm. "Charles, I think your carriage would be best. That way Mr. Hurst can take Caroline home in ours."

Mr. Bingley opened his mouth to respond, but Darcy interrupted. "Whatever carriage is decided upon—and I would gladly offer one of mine, as well—we first need to reach Darcy House. Let us start in that direction; any necessary arrangements can be made on the way."

Causing a mix of exasperation and relief, for Elizabeth longed to speak with Mr. Darcy while simultaneously dreading such a situation, Mrs. Hurst kept her arm hooked through Elizabeth's as they made their way back through the park. She was a woman capable of pleasant conversation when bothered to make an effort, and for the first time Elizabeth found herself as the recipient of Louisa Hurst's energies. She did not quite know what to make of the change.

This seemingly fair-weather friend would have been little more than an amusement had Louisa not leaned close and murmured, "I must apologize for Caroline. I have attempted to make her see sense, but she will not be swayed from her convictions. For her entire life, she has been given everything she ever wanted, and I do not think she knows how to deal with rejection or disappointment." The woman sighed. "And, I suppose, I must apologize for myself as well. I did not care for yourself or your sisters when we were introduced, and I was not happy with the idea of Charles marrying Jane. He could have made a better social match, and we must be aware of that, coming from trade as we do. But any fool can see they are made for each other, and your sister is a dear. I hope you can forgive me, even if you cannot excuse Caroline."

The sentiments relayed in the speech reminded Elizabeth strongly of the relationship between Kitty and Lydia. Lydia, while two years Kitty's junior, had always been the leader of the pair. Unfortunately, she had often lead Kitty into silly intrigues and poor behavior. It took little imagination to apply the same idea to Caroline and Louisa, and Lizzy had not forgotten how much Kitty improved once removed from Lydia's influence.

"Of course I can forgive you, Louisa. It is not wrong for you to want better for your family." And the elder Bingley sister had not tried to push her in front of a horse.

Mrs. Hurst gave her a brilliant smile. "I should have known you would be too sweet, since you are related to Jane."

At that, Elizabeth laughed aloud. "Now you have resorted to false flattery, for my temperament is nothing compared to Jane's. I am fair, I believe, and do my best to be generally good, but to call me sweet is a gross exaggeration. Shall I remind you of my penchant for teasing and arguing?"

Mrs. Hurst laughed as well. "Very well. May I call you pleasant and lively?"

"I believe I can accept those descriptors."

Mrs. Hurst squeezed Elizabeth's arm, then began to talk about her favorite stores in London. The conversation lasted until they reached Darcy House, and contained so many invitations for Jane and Elizabeth to go shopping while in Town that

Elizabeth could only shake her head and wonder if she was truly awake at all, or if the entire expedition had been nothing more than a dream.

Only when Mr. Darcy handed her into the carriage, holding onto her hand for a heartbeat too long and looking at her with eyes that seemed to stare into her very soul, did Elizabeth decide she could not be dreaming. Surely no fantasy, however imaginative, could evoke the same feelings as *that*.

Chapter Twenty

"Don't even think about pretending to be asleep. I know you better than that. If I'm still awake, you definitely are."

Elizabeth rolled over at Jane's whisper. "Would I do that?"

"Hmmm," Jane said. It was too dark to see, but Elizabeth knew her sister was pursing her lips. "You did several things today that I wouldn't have believed if I hadn't seen them with my own eyes. Like holding a sincere conversation with Louisa Hurst for a quarter of an hour. And swooning against Mr. Darcy rather than arguing with him."

Elizabeth shot into a seated position. "I did not *swoon*."

"Hush, or you'll wake up Prissy and have to tell her the story too." Their cousin had the room next door.

"What makes you think there is anything to tell? Other than the fact that Caroline Bingley tried to push me in front of a horse and Mr. Darcy caught me before I was trampled?"

"Yes, but Elizabeth, you *let* him. You didn't storm away, you didn't come up with a joke to turn the attention from you. Instead, you stayed there long enough that I could see you looking around while he held you against him."

"I was disoriented!"

"And when have you *ever*, in your entire life, let someone help you if you could manage on your own? Do you remember how mad you used to get when Hannah would come to help us dress because you could do it yourself—even if you missed half the buttons and got the ties all wrong? What about the time you sprained your ankle and John Lucas tried to carry you home without asking first? You limped the entire way all on your own, just to prove that you could. I still don't know how you managed it."

"Jane—" Elizabeth stopped, unsure of how to continue.

"Lizzy, how long have you loved him?"

At that quiet question, Elizabeth lost all of her fight. "I don't know," she replied after a long pause. "I didn't fully realize my feelings until today. I spent so much time actively hating him that it took the months of separation for me to make any headway into my true emotions. And Lydia's elopement made me consider all of the things I had taken for granted. You cannot be more surprised than I was to realize that Mr. Darcy's company was on the list of things I would miss the most."

Jane gave a light laugh. "Does he know that?"

"I don't know," Elizabeth said again. "I alluded to it in the letter I sent Georgiana after Lydia ran away, and I know he's seen part of what I wrote there. But Jane, I treated him so horribly, so unfairly, I can't see how he could still care for me even if he did know. And I cannot forget how much he abhors Mr. Wickham. If he married me, they would be brothers. He told me very plainly before that he had fought his feelings for me because of my connections—that is even more of a concern now."

Jane sat up as well and turned so they were facing each other. At that angle, Elizabeth could just make out her sister's face in the moonlight from the window. "Lizzy, you should see how he looks at you. But I do not understand. Why has Mr. Darcy read a letter you sent to his sister? How did you come to send it in the first place? Surely you did not write to tell Miss Darcy about Lydia's situation?"

"I did," Elizabeth whispered. She took a deep breath and let it out slowly.

"Lizzy, how could you?"

"Jane, it's what saved them. It's what saved *us*."

"I still don't understand."

"No, how could you? There are still things that I don't know, but— Jane, it isn't all my story, and I'm not supposed to know any of it."

"But you do, and Lydia is my sister, too."

Lizzy took another deep breath. "Very well. I'll tell you my part of the story, with as much detail as I know."

ℰ

The following morning, Elizabeth had just finished her breakfast when a maid delivered a letter. Quite familiar with Georgiana's handwriting after their months of correspondence, Elizabeth had no trouble identifying who the letter was from, and opened it immediately.

Miss Elizabeth,

I beg your forgiveness for the late notice, but I am writing to invite you and Miss Bennet for an outing at Hyde Park early this afternoon. In discussing yesterday's events with my brother, we both feel that a second attempt is required. Mr. and Mrs.

205

*Hurst and Miss Bingley have prior
plans and will be unable to join our
party, but my brother and Mr. Bingley
will be present, and we may also be
able to introduce you to my cousin,
Colonel Fitzwilliam.*

*If this plan is undesirable to you or
your sister, or if you have a previous
commitment, let me know at once. If I
do not hear from you, we shall stop at
your aunt and uncle's house at 2 PM
this afternoon in our carriage.*

Most sincerely,

Georgiana Darcy

Elizabeth hurried up the stairs to find Jane putting
the finishing touches on her hair. Dropping the letter
on the table in front of her, she asked, "What would
you say to another outing at Hyde Park?"

Jane placed the last two pins in her hair, shook her
head to test their hold, and then picked up the letter.
"I don't know if it would be in your best interest to
accept, Lizzy. Another trip to the park could prove
dangerous to you."

Elizabeth laughed. "When did you learn to
tease?" she asked, sitting down on a stool next to

Jane's and tucking a stray curl back into her sister's hair.

"Am I teasing? If so, I can see why you do it. I always thought of teasing as making fun, but that is not necessarily the case, is it?" Her face turned sober. "I am glad Caroline will not be there. It pains me to think of how she acted. Lizzy, are you sure it wasn't an accident?"

"Oh, dear Jane. I know it is hard for you to believe that not everyone in the world is as good as you, but that is the truth. Caroline Bingley pushed me, and she meant to do so. For your sake, I hope you can make peace with her, but do not trust her. She has proven that her own ambitions mean more than the well-being of others. I would be happy to never see her again, but I will survive as long as she does not stand too close when there are green-broke horses nearby." Realizing what she had said, Elizabeth gave a short laugh. "I suppose I should say, I will survive both figuratively *and* literally, although I only meant in the figurative sense."

Jane still looked pained, but she did not argue. "Well, an outing would be pleasant. I would like to get to know Miss Darcy better. We did not have much of an opportunity to converse yesterday." She picked up the note and reread it. "And I wonder what Colonel Fitzwilliam is like."

Elizabeth doubted her sister would be truly aware of anyone besides Mr. Bingley, but she kept that thought to herself. Aloud, she said, "I suppose we shall find out. Come; Prissy has been wanting to visit the shops with us and there is enough time to do so if we go now."

"Lizzy? Are you happy that you will see Mr. Darcy again?"

Yes. "I think I'll see how today goes before I decide. You can quiz me again tonight."

"I will!" Jane exclaimed and, laughing, they left in search of their cousin.

&

The carriage pulled up just as the clocks were striking two. Darcy, Bingley, and Georgiana emerged, Georgiana looking around herself with obvious curiosity. Elizabeth, watching from a window, wondered briefly how Mr. Darcy felt about his precious little sister standing on a street in Cheapside. Then she took a closer look at the party and realized that he seemed more relaxed in his current setting than he had in Netherfield's ballroom. Mr. Darcy had acted very different during their time together in London, and she certainly thought of him in a different light—why could she not accept this change as well?

The visitors were welcomed warmly, and they spent several minutes conversing with Mrs. Gardiner before returning to the waiting carriage, this time with Jane and Elizabeth as well. The ladies settled themselves on one of the benches, across from the gentlemen, and Elizabeth found herself tucked between Jane and Georgiana. That part of the situation left her quite comfortable, and indeed put her in mind of carriage rides with her sisters. The fact that she faced Mr. Darcy directly was harder to accept with serenity.

To keep from staring at the man or teasing him to break the tension, Elizabeth turned to Georgiana. "You mentioned in your letter that your cousin might be joining us. Is that not the case?"

"Oh, Richard—Colonel Fitzwilliam—will be meeting us there," Georgiana said. "It will be wonderful to see him again; he has not been on leave for months, and even when he is in London there are still a great deal of social events that he is required to attend."

"It must be difficult for him as well, not being able to make decisions based solely on what he wishes to do with his time."

Darcy made a noise dangerously close to a snort. "Do not let her sell you a tale of woe, Miss Elizabeth. My cousin greatly enjoys those social events. I have often thought it would make more sense if he were related to Bingley than to me."

Hearing his name, Bingley managed to turn from Jane. "The colonel is a most entertaining guest. We must have dinner while he is in Town—that way you can sit in silence and enjoy a meal where no one expects you to speak, Darce." He looked at Georgiana, and Elizabeth realized that Bingley had been paying more attention to the conversation than she had given him credit for. "It will be a small party, which makes it a social event that you can attend as well."

Georgiana smiled shyly, reminding Elizabeth of Darcy's comment. "I have found the difference between myself and my siblings remarkable at times, so I cannot express any great surprise that your cousin is fonder of social events than you. In any case, he sounds like an interesting man, and I look forward to meeting him."

Darcy frowned. "I am sure you will find him agreeable; nearly everyone does." The words were polite, but Elizabeth heard the undertone. Was Colonel Fitzwilliam another individual to whom Darcy was compared, much like Bingley and Wickham? It would grow old to always find yourself the quiet, stern, and less entertaining person.

The thought made Elizabeth furious, with a ferocity that took her by surprise. She hated the look of desolation that had flashed across Darcy's face as he spoke, even though it was now well covered. "We have discussed temperaments before, but I would renew the subject now. What do you think, Mr. Darcy—does being agreeable carry more weight than intelligent conversation or constancy?"

He arched one eyebrow. "I believe you can predict my answer, Miss Elizabeth. Are you truly asking for my opinion or stating your own?"

"I always ask for your true opinion, Mr. Darcy. That does not mean I will not challenge you if I disagree."

Bingley gave a theatrical moan. "Not again," he said, shooting Elizabeth a smile before he looked back at Jane. "When you and Miss Elizabeth stayed with us at Netherfield, all they did in the evenings was read or argue—mostly argue. When she could be spared from your bedside, of course."

"Ah, so now the truth comes out," Jane said, her usual sweet smile given more flavor by the new teasing light in her eyes. "Lizzy made it sound as if the evenings consisted of your sisters performing on the pianoforte while you and Mr. Darcy played chess."

Elizabeth glanced over at Georgiana and noticed that the younger girl was taking in the conversation with wide eyes. "Do you argue with your brother, Miss Darcy?"

"Oh, no," Georgiana exclaimed. "I could never argue with Fitzwilliam."

Hoping she wasn't blushing as she considered his given name but determined to ask nonetheless, Elizabeth looked back at Mr. Darcy. "That reminds me, I have been wondering. Your cousin is Colonel Fitzwilliam—are your names related?" Well, she'd made a tangle of those words, hadn't she!

Luckily, Darcy didn't appear to have noticed her fluster. "They are. My mother was a Fitzwilliam, and I am named for her family." The carriage slowed, and Darcy looked out the window. "And it appears that Colonel Fitzwilliam is already here." He gave Elizabeth an almost-smile that showed more in his eyes than his mouth. "I shall look forward to hearing your opinions on my cousin."

Chapter Twenty-One

Bingley exited the carriage first, turning back to help Jane down and tucking her arm securely into his once her feet had touched the ground. Darcy was left to help Georgiana and Elizabeth from the carriage. The former went directly to Colonel Fitzwilliam; the latter stayed where she was, watching Mr. Darcy as he watched his sister.

"I wonder if you actually want my opinion on your cousin, or if you simply thought that was the correct thing to say," Elizabeth commented, mirroring his words from earlier.

The corner of Darcy's mouth quirked as he looked away from Georgiana, but it did not appear to be a happy expression. "Everyone likes my cousin, Miss Elizabeth. *I* like my cousin, which can be said about very few people of my acquaintance."

Elizabeth laughed. "That is very high praise indeed."

He smiled wryly. "You have an opinion on everyone; I remember your comments on myself most vividly. And since you have surprised me with your views on multiple occasions and subjects, then yes, I am truly interested in hearing your thoughts."

She had hardly been complimentary when expressing her views on him. Surely he knew that her opinions had changed—but perhaps not. Would he have brought it up if he didn't know her disdain was a thing of the past? Or were his words meant to convey a message she had missed? Elizabeth didn't know, and it frustrated her. There had not been an opportunity to talk privately since she had arrived in London, and even if there was, Elizabeth did not know what she would say.

Something about how he looked at his cousin pulled at her emotions, though, and she could not brush the moment aside. It was as she had thought in the carriage. He expected her to rejoice in the new, *agreeable* acquaintance and disregard his presence, maybe even ignore him outright. How many people had done that, not only with Colonel Fitzwilliam, but with Bingley and Wickham? Steeling herself in case she was wrong, Elizabeth reached out and placed a hand on Darcy's arm. "Then perhaps you should introduce me. There will be time to discuss my observations while we walk."

He jerked slightly when she touched him, eyes falling to where her fingers lay on his sleeve. When he looked back up at her, his expressions were masked, but she could swear she had seen something akin to hope flare in his eyes.

All he said, though, was, "If you insist, Miss Elizabeth."

"Darcy!" Colonel Fitzwilliam exclaimed as they approached. "I am astonished to see you out of your study. Have you decided at long last to explore the great outdoors?"

Elizabeth glanced up at Mr. Darcy and realized that while he wasn't smiling, exactly, his face made it clear that his cousin's teasing did not bother him. He really *did* like the other man, and his next comment made that fact even more clear. "Your memory must be going, old man. I recall spending a great deal of time exploring the outdoors with you when we were children."

"Ah, but that was at Pemberley, or when we were able to escape from Lady Catherine at Rosings. I have long assumed that you come to Town only to hibernate."

Elizabeth attempted to turn a snort into a cough with marginal success, drawing the attention of both men.

"Miss Elizabeth, may I present my cousin, Colonel Richard Fitzwilliam of His Majesty's army? Richard, this is Miss Elizabeth Bennet of Longbourn, in Hertfordshire." Looking amused, Darcy added, "She is a great walker, and having met our dear aunt, I am sure she can understand the desire to escape into the outdoors when given the chance."

The colonel's eyebrows shot up his forehead, and he gave Darcy a quick look before turning back to Elizabeth and bowing; Elizabeth dipped into a curtsey in return. "A pleasure to make your acquaintance, Miss Elizabeth. I feel as though there is a story at hand—forgive my candor, but how did you come to make the acquaintance of Lady Catherine?"

Elizabeth could not help the glance she sent Mr. Darcy, realizing only after she found him looking at her as well how it must appear to his cousin. Giving the colonel a wry smile, she said, "My cousin, Mr. Collins, is Lady Catherine's rector. He recently came to stay with my family, and during his visit my father fell suddenly ill." Prepared this time, she managed to keep from glancing at Mr. Darcy yet again as she recalled the events surrounding her father's collapse. "Lady Catherine came to, well, let us say she came to offer her assistance through advice. She did not stay long, but she made quite the impact during her time at Longbourn."

Colonel Fitzwilliam laughed. "I have no trouble believing that!" Losing his jovial look, he added, "Your father has recovered, I hope?"

"He has; thank you for your concern."

"And is your whole family in town?"

"No, only myself and my elder sister, Jane." Elizabeth nodded to where Jane and Bingley stood nearby, talking. "My parents and two of my younger sisters remain at our home in Netherfield." She instantly regretted the comment, because there would be no avoiding a mention of Lydia now.

"Two of your younger sisters?" Colonel Fitzwilliam laughed again. "How many are there?"

"There are five of us in all," Elizabeth told him. "My youngest sister was recently married and is no longer at home." She steadfastly refused to look at Darcy or Georgiana, focusing on keeping a pleasant smile on her face instead.

"My goodness, four sisters! Do you have any brothers?"

Perhaps they could avoid the topic of Lydia after all. "No, there are only the five of us. Mr. Collins is to inherit Longbourn, you see, which might explain some of Lady Catherine's interest in our family matters."

The colonel gave Darcy another look, one that Elizabeth did not even attempt to understand. "Perhaps," he said.

Jane and Bingley came over then and Bingley introduced Jane with a pride that spoke volumes. Colonel Fitzwilliam greeted them both pleasantly, then looked around at the group as a whole. "Shall we walk? I am still not convinced that Darcy is capable of such a mundane, social activity." He held out his arm towards Elizabeth, but before she could react Georgiana stepped forward.

"It is so good to see you again," she exclaimed in a voice that Elizabeth, having become accustomed to her usual quiet tones, realized was exuberantly loud for Georgiana. "How long are you in Town? Will you be going to Rosings for Easter, or to Matlock?"

Bingley immediately offered Jane his arm, and she took it with a smile. Left behind, Darcy and Elizabeth looked at each other; Elizabeth still wearing her pleasant façade and Darcy with a quizzical smile. After a moment's hesitation, he bowed slightly to Elizabeth. "Shall we, Miss Elizabeth?"

"Of course. We can't allow your cousin to think that the activity is beyond your capabilities." She took his arm with no prompting, and they followed the others.

"My cousin has often observed me in the presence of Miss Bingley and her ilk. He is not wrong about my social skills when such people are present."

Elizabeth laughed. "You forget, I was also present at Netherfield when the rain kept us all indoors. You once managed to spend the entire afternoon in my presence without saying a single word, and you always seemed to have a book or letter at hand for distraction. I was impressed at your relative success in avoiding conversation, since Miss Bingley's main goal seemed to be gaining any of your attention."

Darcy stopped abruptly and turned to face Elizabeth. "How can you discuss her so calmly? I cannot think of her without—" he broke off and looked away, composing himself before he continued. "What happened yesterday has been repeating over and over in my mind. If I had not been able to pull you back in time—" He stopped again.

Elizabeth waited until it seemed sure that he would not go on. "We are both lucky that you did," she said, making her voice as lighthearted as she could manage and feeling like she had utterly failed. "Do not think of what might have been. It is past, and I am unharmed—something I must add to my list of things for which I am in your debt." So much for being light-hearted! Well, she had other serious things to say as well. Elizabeth took a deep breath and continued, "It is past time I thanked you, sir, not only for myself but for Lydia and my family as well. If my family knew what you had done for Lydia— and thus for all of us—I would have more than my own gratitude to relay."

Darcy shook his head, although Elizabeth did not know exactly what he was negating. "I will not ask how you came to know that. Your family owes me nothing; as much I am glad I was able to help, I thought only of *you*. And however much I might agree with the logic of your words, I cannot keep myself from thinking of yesterday. If I had reacted just an instant later—I could not have borne it."

They had entered a tree-covered lane with few other people, and it was easy to imagine they were alone when Darcy led her into the shadow of a large oak on the edge of the path. "Miss Elizabeth, I was a fool when I spoke to you in Hertfordshire. I have regretted it for months, but in following the rules of society I saw little that I could do, and I was afraid to open myself up to rejection once again. After yesterday, I cannot stay silent. Rejection is nothing compared to the fear I felt when I thought—"

Darcy stopped, jaw clenching, and Elizabeth knew he was fighting to regain his control. "You are too generous to trifle with me," he went on after a moment. "If you feel as you did in November, tell me so at once. My feelings and wishes have not changed. One word from you will silence me forever, but I cannot let any more time pass without speaking."

Elizabeth opened her mouth and found that she could not speak. She stared up at Darcy, still not sure she had heard him correctly. He had been polite and paid her attention while she was in Town, but despite Jane's teasing and assurances otherwise she had never expected this. Not with how she had treated him in Hertfordshire. Not now that Mr. Wickham was her brother.

In her confusion, she tightened her grip on Darcy's arm and thought she saw some of the anxiety leave his eyes in response. But she would not keep him in suspense, and so forced herself to speak, although she could not manage to do so while meeting his eyes. "I—I would not wish to silence you. I—you were not the only fool, Mr. Darcy, and I knew regret the instant I understood the truth of the situation."

"I should have told you myself," he said, something in his voice that she had never heard before.

"But would I have listened? I was proud of the opinion I had formed, proud of my judgement of character, incorrect though it was, and I read Georgiana's letter multiple times before I began to accept it as truth." Elizabeth glanced up, then away again. "No matter how it came about, or what could have been done differently, my feelings are incomparable to what they were in November, and your words now bring me great—" she flushed brilliantly— "great pleasure and gratitude."

"Elizabeth," he said reverently, the tone of his voice causing goosebumps to break out on her arms. If she had any lingering doubts about Mr. Darcy's feelings, they soon disappeared as he continued to speak, and while Elizabeth could still not bring herself to meet his eyes, nothing prevented her from listening intently.

They walked on absently, with no thought of the others in their party or indeed anyone else in the park. There was too much to be thought, and felt, and said, for attention to any other objects. Events were reexamined without the taint of prejudice and comments were clarified. Elizabeth explained how she had become aware of Darcy's involvement in Lydia's marriage, and in turn asked if he had known of Georgiana's letter before it was sent.

At that question, he laughed. "I knew nothing about it, and I have wondered for months what inspired her to send it. When she ran into my study waving your reply and talking incoherently about Mr. Wickham and needing to help, you could have knocked me over with a feather. I'm still not sure how I managed to hide my surprise, although it certainly helped that Georgiana was in a large amount of distress." He frowned. "I do not usually consider that a desirable state." Another hesitation. "Did you think I had put her up to it?"

"No," Elizabeth answered slowly. "I wondered, when the letter first arrived, but after reading it I could not imagine that you would approve. I spent a good deal more time attempting to figure out what Georgiana hoped to accomplish."

"I ought to scold her, but I cannot do so in good conscience. I am far too pleased with the results of her interference. Without her, your sister would not have been located, and even if you came to London under different circumstances, I never would have known you were here."

"She has certainly been helpful," Elizabeth agreed with a laugh. "I may have to ask her for advice, for I have my own letter to write." Seeing Darcy's raised brow, she clarified. "My father. I will have to work to make him believe that I am not joking."

"Will he be unhappy?" Darcy asked immediately, his concern obvious.

"Not if he believes *I* am happy," she replied. "But you see, I was rather vocal in my dislike of you this past fall, and my father was not privy to the information that changed my opinion."

Darcy actually blushed. "Your father and I spoke—once—while he was at Netherfield. He may be less surprised than you believe. While Elizabeth processed that comment in stunned silence, Darcy went on, "I have been considering going to visit your father at Longbourn. I would be happy to carry a letter from you, if you would like."

"There they are!" Colonel Fitzwilliam exclaimed from just ahead, and both Darcy and Elizabeth jumped. "We were beginning to worry you were lost."

Darcy hesitated, studying the group ahead. "May I call on you tomorrow?" he asked, ignoring his cousin.

Elizabeth smiled. "I would like that very much."

Chapter Twenty-Two

Three days later found a very distracted Elizabeth sitting with needlework forgotten on her lap while she watched the street outside her aunt and uncle's house for a tall man on a dark horse.

"You know, Lizzy, staring won't bring him any sooner," Jane remarked in an impish tone. "A watched pot never boils, after all."

Elizabeth fixed her sister with a stern look, then ruined the effect by glancing out the window once again. "You have no reason to doubt Mr. Bingley's reception," she said. "Don't chastise me for worrying just because you are secure in your happiness." Jane had teased her relentlessly since the day Mr. Darcy proposed, and while Elizabeth enjoyed many of their conversations, she did not appreciate the joke with butterflies churning in her stomach.

"Perhaps next time you will hold your tongue rather than passing judgement so publicly on a stranger!" Jane exclaimed now. "You have no one to blame but yourself, Lizzy. And you know Papa will not deny you if it is truly what you want."

Elizabeth did not doubt the truth of Jane's words, but it did little to keep her from worrying. The thought that she would make her father unhappy with her choice had kept her up for the better part of the last two nights, made even worse by the admittedly unreasonable thought of him collapsing again upon reading her letter. With that in mind, she had done her best to temper her words and introduce the true purpose slowly, but her father was an intelligent man. She could only imagine what he must have thought when Mr. Darcy invaded his study and announced that he carried a letter from her.

In the end, both Mr. Darcy and Mr. Bingley had ridden to Longbourn to ask Mr. Bennet for a daughter's hand in marriage. Anxious as she was, Elizabeth could not help the relief she felt at being far away while her mother processed the news. Fanny Bennet could not ignore even her least favorite daughter when she was to become Mrs. Darcy, and Elizabeth enjoyed few things less than those rare occasions when her mother's nervous energy directed at herself.

"There!" Elizabeth exclaimed, spotting Mr. Darcy in the midst of the bustling street outside the house.

She jumped up, needlework falling to the floor as she hurried out of the room and down the stairs. A knock sounded on the door just as she reached it, and Elizabeth wrenched it open rather than waiting for a servant.

He was backlit by the bright mid-afternoon sun, but she could still see his smile, and it loosened the knots in her stomach even as her heart began to race. Darcy took one large step forward and crushed her against himself. It was only an instant before he stepped back, but Elizabeth felt as if every nerve on her body had burst into flame at the embrace.

She was vaguely aware of Mr. Bingley appearing in the doorway behind Darcy, and both Mrs. Gardiner and Jane coming down the stairs to join the party, but that was all distant compared to Darcy's intense look, and the letter he held out with her name written on it in her father's hand.

"Here," he said, giving her a smile. "You were right in your estimation of his reaction, but do not worry; he believed you."

Darcy bowed to Mrs. Gardiner and Jane, then stepped to the side of the hallway as Elizabeth seized the letter and tore it open.

Lizzy,

I always knew I would have to part with you someday, and after a great deal of contemplation I cannot truly express much surprise at your manner of leaving. Oh, do not doubt that I thought you had taken leave of your senses when Mr. Darcy first handed me your letter, but you know me well. Your letter did much to assuage my worries, and I thank you for taking the time to explain as fully as you did.

I will not keep you in suspense. I have given him my consent. He is the kind of man, indeed, to whom I should never dare refuse anything, which he condescended to ask. I now give it to you, as it seems you are resolved on having him. If what you say is truly the case, he deserves you, and I am not inclined to doubt what is perhaps the most heart-felt letter I have ever received from you. I could not have parted with you, my Lizzy, to anyone less worthy.

As I am sure you have guessed, your mother is much overcome by the news, and since I am uninclined to share all the details of your letter with her, she has spent a good deal of time wondering—loudly—at how her most argumentative daughter caught the richest man of our acquaintance. I believe that she is truly happy for you in her own way, and I do not doubt you will hear a good deal of her feelings from herself when you return home. Mr. Darcy and Mr. Bingley have both agreed to a wedding in Hertfordshire, and I confess I will be happy to have you under my roof once more before you leave for good.

As for your intended, I have spent several hours with him since our first meeting, and he continues to rise in my esteem. Will it upset you to know that I have already been invited to visit Pemberley, and intend to do so before the year is out? If Mr. Darcy's library is half the quality he reports, any remaining reservations I have concerning your marriage will easily be assuaged—I jest, of course.

This may be the time to tell of a most amusing conversation I had last fall— one I half believed to be a dream until today. Your Mr. Darcy was present when I awoke at Netherfield, although I could not say if he was reading to me or simply escaping the company. He expressed a great deal of relief that I was recovering, and stated that it had brought him great distress to think of you being forced into marriage with a man who did not deserve you. When I asked him who did, he grew flustered, and I believe was quite grateful when the nurse arrived to assess my condition.

I will end here, for Mr. Darcy is most anxious to return to London and perhaps more accurately, to you. Please give my most sincere congratulations to Jane, and I look forward to seeing both of you in the near future.

Your loving father,

Thomas Bennet.

Elizabeth read the letter twice in rapid succession, then a third time to make sure she had not misunderstood anything. Finally convinced of her father's approval, she looked up to find Mr. Darcy watching her with a smile.

"You were worried?" he asked in an undertone, stepping closer so they could talk with the semblance of privacy even as Jane and Mr. Bingley conversed with Mrs. Gardiner just down the hall.

She smiled, relief and excitement combining to make her feel giddy. "It was silly, perhaps, but I was. I have always been my father's favorite, and it distressed me greatly to think that I would cause him pain, especially after his episode last fall."

"So you were only worried for him?"

Elizabeth jerked back, then gave a short laugh. "Mr. Darcy, teasing? Who is this creature? No, sir, I was not only worried for him. I was worried he would not believe me and refuse you, and I was equally worried that he *would* believe me but give you a hard time all the same. I love my father, but he can be stubborn to a fault in his teasing, and ours is the sort of situation at which he loves to poke fun."

"Come, let us go into the sitting room," Mrs. Gardiner said, placing a hand on Elizabeth's shoulder as she passed. "Mr. Darcy, does this mean my niece will have a chance to become better acquainted with the Derbyshire wilds?"

Elizabeth laughed, thinking back to the first awkward conversation she had had with Mr. Darcy upon her arrival in London. "I believe you promised me a guide, Mr. Darcy," she teased.

"You will explore whether you know the lay of land or not, so I believe a guide will be the first item of business upon our arrival," he told her. Looking up at Mrs. Gardiner, he continued, "Indeed it does. I hope you will join us at Pemberley soon; if I recall correctly, Mr. Gardiner is fond of fishing, and we have several ideal fishing holes whose occupants are left in peace far too much of the time."

Elizabeth had a sudden vision of Mr. Darcy as he had looked when they first met—cold, aloof, and distinctly unhappy to be socializing with those of a lower class. Had someone told her he would invite her Uncle Gardiner to fish at his estate in less than a year, she would have accused them of overindulging in the punch. Then again, had someone said she would be overjoyed to become Mrs. Darcy, her reaction would have been the same. It seemed that love—and true understanding—could do much to change a person.

ε

Of all the reactions Elizabeth received once the news of her engagement spread, Georgiana's was by far the sweetest. Elizabeth and Jane called at Darcy House the day after Mr. Darcy returned from Hertfordshire, and no sooner had the door closed behind them were they greeted by a streak of white muslin and lace racing down the stairs. Georgiana checked herself just short of the guests and managed to catch her balance long enough to curtsey. Then she caught hold of Elizabeth's hands and bounced up and down on the balls of her feet.

Looking over the younger girl's shoulder, Elizabeth caught sight of Darcy, standing in the doorway to his study, mouth covered with his fist as he fought back laughter. She gave him a quizzical look until she realized Georgiana's greeting was almost identical to her reaction the day before, then joined in the laughter. Pulling Georgiana in close, Elizabeth gave her a tight hug.

"Thank you," she whispered in her new sister's ear.

"I knew I was right to send that letter," Georgiana whispered back. "Oh, Elizabeth, I am so happy."

"I think you had better call me Lizzy," Elizabeth responded. "After all, that is how all my other sisters refer to me."

Georgiana pulled back, and Elizabeth could tell from her expression that she had been hoping for such an invitation, even if she never would have hinted at it left to her own devices. "I cannot believe I will have a sister at last."

"You may grow to regret it," Elizabeth teased. "I know there were times growing up when I would have been happy to give away a sister or two—or even three!" She shot Jane a grin. "There were likely days when Jane wished to be rid of all four of us, although she is too kind to ever admit it."

"Oh Lizzy, of course not," Jane exclaimed. "I can't image growing up without all of you, and I certainly wouldn't want to."

"See?" Elizabeth asked Georgiana. "She is too good to be real. I believe Mr. Bingley has the right of it when he calls her an angel, for only a heavenly creature could put up with four obnoxious younger sisters who always wanted her to braid their hair and loan them clothes and settle arguments and speak of the experience with fondness."

Mr. Darcy left his doorway and approached the group. "Shall we continue to the drawing room?" he asked. Not waiting for an answer, he held out his arm to Elizabeth and motioned for Jane and Georgiana to proceed them up the stairs. Once they were a little way ahead, he gave her a crooked smile and murmured, "I believe Georgiana created a great deal of alarm when she saw you. Many of the servants here have never heard her shriek the way she did when your carriage pulled up. I don't think *I've* heard it since she was a little girl. It would always give me away when I tried to sneak her sweets."

Elizabeth lifted an eyebrow. "If I ever hear Georgiana shriek, I will react with alarm as well. I hope this is not an indication of how much I am to disrupt your peaceful household."

Darcy stopped, which effectively stopped Elizabeth as well. "I disagree. I very much hope you

234

will continue disrupting *our* household in such a way. What you call peaceful has been in truth somber for far too long, and I am delighted to see how your liveliness brightens the entire house."

Elizabeth leaned close and mock whispered, "Is this a bad time to admit that I used to have a very strong propensity for sliding down banisters such as this?" She reached out and ran a hand over the gleaming mahogany rail at her side.

Darcy rocked back and laughed, sounding less guarded than she had ever heard him. He ran a hand over his face while she watched, bemused. "My Lord, Elizabeth."

She was still unaccustomed to his use of her Christian name, and she had just enough time to register it and blush when he went on, "I will keep your secret if you do not tell anyone that Colonel Fitzwilliam and I once gained a pair of bloody noses by racing down this very banister. Lady Catherine was present, and my father had to take us to his office for our punishment because he kept laughing at how horrified she was."

They turned together and continued up the stairs. "And will the great lady be horrified when our news reaches her?" Elizabeth asked with a twinge of trepidation at the thought of disrupting her betrothed's family.

"Certainly," Darcy responded calmly. "But she will recover in time, and I am sure you will find a way to paint her actions in a humorous light when she cannot be avoided." He leaned close again and murmured, "You see, I intend to keep you to myself for at least a year. Perhaps I shall learn to share with Georgiana, but I must insist that all other family leave us in peace for a time."

"We'll bring Kitty to Pemberley so Georgiana has a companion closer to her age," Elizabeth smiled back. "They can distract each other."

"You, my dear, are a genius," Darcy told her. "I do believe they will get along together very well— and so will we."

Elizabeth beamed up at him. It was wonderful to know she could joke so freely with her soon-to-be-husband as well as debating with him. Yes, she was going to enjoy being Mrs. Darcy very much indeed.

There was something magical about Pemberley, Elizabeth thought, that brought out the best in every season. The entire countryside came alive in the spring, summer brought the perfect shade of emerald green, and fall turned the foliage into a painting. Even winter, her least favorite season with its propensity to keep one trapped indoors, created a landscape fit for a fairy queen.

It was winter tonight, and the full moon lit up the world outside Elizabeth's window in a way that brought out all of the beauty without the blinding glare of the daytime sun. She had wrapped a dressing gown around herself to ward of the chill and been staring out at the tableau for an indeterminate amount of time when a voice came from behind her.

"I thought you were going to bed hours ago."

Elizabeth didn't turn. He had found her like this enough times that she knew what came next, and sure enough in the next moment arms wrapped around her from behind. She leaned back into the broad expanse of her husband's chest with a happy sigh.

"I could say the same of you," she replied, nestling closer and turning her head slightly so it was tucked under his chin. "The light was too bright, and I got up to close the curtains better. Somehow, this was more enticing than my bed. I can sleep late tomorrow."

"Not if this little one has anything to say about it," he said, running a hand over the swell of her midsection. "How are you feeling?"

Elizabeth fought back the urge to roll her eyes. "Really, between you and Georgiana, I'll have heard that question more than my own name soon. She asked me that three times after dinner and came by to check on me again before she went to bed."

"Can you blame us if we want you to be happy?" Darcy asked. "You have brought so much joy to our lives it is hard to see you in any sort of distress."

The low rumble of his voice did not conceal the worry she knew he was trying to hide, and so she gave an honest answer rather than teasing. "I am well. Truly. We are past the most trying part, and I've felt much better this time than with Margaret." She peeked up at him with an impish grin. "My mother tells me I should assure you that is a sign of a boy, although since she only had girls I am not sure I trust her expertise."

Her first pregnancy had been extremely hard, and Elizabeth had greeted the news that she was expecting her second child with mixed emotions. To her extreme gratification, this pregnancy brought only mild morning sickness, and now in her sixth month, Elizabeth felt as healthy as ever.

"I wouldn't mind a boy," Darcy remarked, kissing her temple. "Then again, I would be just as happy with another girl, although a boy would certainly even out the ratio in the house. You, Margaret, Georgiana, and Kitty have me outnumbered."

"I don't think we'll have to worry about Georgiana or Kitty for much longer," Elizabeth mused. "Georgiana may have let it slip that she is actually looking forward to Lady Adair's ball, and I know it can only be for a reason named *Henry*. Has he talked to you yet?"

Darcy sighed. "He hasn't officially, but we've been having a series of conversations over the past two months that are leading in that direction. I have far more sympathy for your father now than I used to. Maybe it would be better if this little one *is* a boy. I'm struggling with the idea that Georgiana is old enough to marry; the thought of giving Margaret away is enough to keep me up at night."

"I think you have a bit of time to get used to the idea," Elizabeth told him. "Margaret is two, but Georgiana is nineteen, and she is ready for her own home. Lord Westbrook will be a good match for her, and in far more ways than status. Kitty has helped bring her out of her shell, but Georgiana will never be outgoing, and Lord Westbrook helps her in public without forcing to be someone she isn't."

Darcy pulled her even closer to him. "I won't say you are wrong, but don't expect me to like it." He paused. "Are *you* looking forward to Lady Adair's ball, Lizzy? And didn't she just hold a ball?"

Elizabeth laughed. Lady Adair, née Caroline Bingley, had continued to slight Elizabeth whenever possible. As long as she kept her distance, Elizabeth found it amusing, especially since it meant she was not required to make small talk with the woman. "She did, but if I were married to Lord Adair I would distract myself from him as much as possible, too. Besides, it is her money—he can't complain too much about how she spends it. As to your other question, I am looking forward to seeing Jane. It is much harder to find time for each other now, and I cherish any time that we have together. Do you know if Anne and Richard will be present? I would like to see them as well."

The thought of the couple always made Elizabeth smile. Anne de Bourgh's first words to Elizabeth had been to thank her for taking Darcy off the marriage market. It forced Lady Catherine to listen to her daughter for once, and Anne was finally married to the man she loved. Elizabeth had never known the sickly, listless woman her husband described, but she had been glad to learn that Anne did not harbor feelings for Darcy. According to everyone who had known her, Anne was much livelier than before, and her health had improved greatly under her husband's doting care. Elizabeth knew only that she had gained a sound friend in her new cousin. As for Colonel Fitzwilliam, the marriage had given him a home and income that would let him retire from the army as well as a wife that he loved. They were frequent visitors at Darcy House when Darcy and Elizabeth were in London and occasionally came to Pemberley as well.

"I believe so," Darcy said. "Richard's last letter said they were planning on attending, assuming he is in Town and Anne is well. I may have forgotten to tell you, he has also invited us to Rosings this summer. Originally, he asked if we would come for Easter, but traveling will be out of the question then, and I have always found Rosings to be most pleasant in the summer anyhow."

"Has Lady Catherine finally deigned to allow my presence?" Elizabeth asked.

Darcy chuckled. He picked up her and settled both of them on the window seat before answering. "From the hints that Richard put in his letter, I think

Anne told her mother you would be coming and didn't pay her any attention until she quit screeching. She may have also refused to let Lady Catherine see little Lewis, but Richard didn't say enough on that for me to be sure."

Elizabeth shifted on Darcy's lap so she could see his face. "Lady Catherine, a doting grandmother. I never would have guessed. Well, I'm sure whatever Anne did will somehow be my fault, but I am glad we are to visit them—if you mean to go, that is. I would dearly love to see Charlotte, too."

"If you want to go and are well, we will go."

"My, but aren't you an accommodating husband," Elizabeth teased. "Whatever did you do with that stern, unapproving man I met? Imagine how stunned he would be if he could see you now!"

He kissed her cheek, starting just below her ear and working his way slowly down her jaw until at last his mouth found hers. Elizabeth shivered in response and he pulled her closer. Moving back just far enough to rest his forehead on hers, Darcy murmured, "He would be jealous."

"Hmm? Oh, really? I was under the impression that I couldn't even tempt him into a single dance."

He kissed her again, taking his time. Elizabeth lost herself in the sensation, and when Darcy pulled away and whispered, "You have no idea how jealous," it took her a moment to remember what he was talking about.

"Well," she said once her mind caught up, "I guess he's lucky, then, isn't he?"

"Imp," he said with a smile, kissing her nose. She instinctively raised her face for a real kiss, but he pulled back, laughing quietly.

"You know, if we visit Rosings, you'll have to see Mr. Collins," Elizabeth told him.

"Is this how you pay me back for not kissing you?" Darcy asked. She just grinned at him, and he gave a rueful smile. "As long as Mr. Collins keeps a good distance from my wife—say, at least in another room—I think I can manage to tolerate the man."

"He's probably still scared of you. Do you think that means he'll be quiet in your presence or just talk more?"

"I was under the impression that it would be impossible for him to talk more. Perhaps—"

Elizabeth stifled a yawn and Darcy stopped talking. "Enough conversation for now. You need rest."

She tucked her head into the hollow at his shoulder. "I can rest here."

"Yes, but you'll be far more comfortable in bed." Not waiting for an answer—and despite the fact that she felt like a swollen heifer—Darcy adjusted his arms around her and lifted her as if she weighed no more than a child. Setting her down on the edge of the bed, he slid the dressing gown off her shoulders and brushed one thumb over the skin it exposed.

"If you're going to make me shiver, you'd better stay to warm me up," she said, tipping her head back to look up at him. Away from the window, the room was dark, but Elizabeth could still see his smile.

"You know I will." Darcy divested himself of trousers and slid in next to her. As she snuggled close and drifted off towards sleep, Elizabeth's mind drifted back to their conversation. Her husband was not the only one who had changed, she thought sleepily. She was still fundamentally the same person, and often thought of herself as Lizzy Bennet rather than Elizabeth Darcy, but the last three years had tempered her emotions.

Darcy's hand found hers beneath the covers, fingers entwining, and Elizabeth smiled in the darkness. He had turned her world—expectations, hopes, prejudices, and all—on its head, but that was one change she would make again in a heartbeat. Pride, after all, was nothing compared to love. And with that thought, Elizabeth Darcy fell asleep.

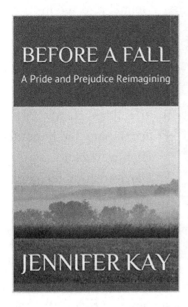

When Mr. Collins makes his awful proposal, Elizabeth runs away - straight into a confrontation between none other than George Wickham and Georgiana Darcy. Elizabeth wants to escape Mr. Collins clutches; Georgiana wants a confidante who understands what she has been through. The friendship that springs up between the two and the resulting events change the course of Jane Austen's best-loved novel. And of course, there is always the question of how a certain stern gentleman will react to his sister's new acquaintance...

Beginning the day after the Netherfield Ball, before a Fall examines what could have happened in Pride and Prejudice if several key events were tweaked slightly. Will Mr. Wickham get his comeuppance? Will Elizabeth and Mr. Darcy find their happily ever after? One thing is certain - pride cometh before a fall.

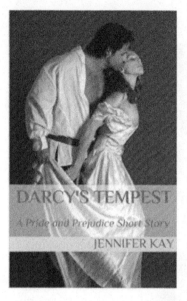

Months after Elizabeth Bennet rejected his proposal, Darcy confesses to Bingley that he was wrong about Jane Bennet's affections. He agrees to accompany the hopeful Bingley back to Hertfordshire, resigned to seeing Elizabeth but with little hope of winning her hand. That all changes when a storm strands them alone together. Can Darcy make the most of the situation and convince Elizabeth that he has changed? Or is he still the last man in the world she could ever be prevailed upon to marry?

This alternate ending to Jane Austen's most beloved story, told from Darcy's perspective, explores what would have happened if Darcy and Elizabeth met again in Hertfordshire rather than at Pemberley. At 10,000+ words, it is a short glimpse into Jane Austen's world that can be enjoyed in an afternoon or evening. E-book only.

About the Author

Jennifer Kay started writing stories in Kindergarten. She rarely got past designing the cover, but the habit stayed with her, and before long the covers turned into short stories and the stories into novels. In college, Jen discovered Pride and Prejudice and it's safe to say life has never been the same. She has a minor in English but primarily writes as an escape from her day job in engineering - and yes, all her coworkers call her crazy. Jen lives a long way from Pemberley with her very own Mr. Darcy and a very regal cat.

Made in the USA
Las Vegas, NV
07 March 2024

86851787R00146